Once at home in sunny Brazil,
Luana DaRosa has since lived on
three different continents—though
her favourite romantic locations
remain the tropical places of Latin
America. When she's not typing
away at her latest romance novel,
or reading about love, Luana is
either crocheting, buying yarn she
doesn't need, or chasing her bunnies
around her house. She lives with her
partner in a cosy town in the south of
England. Find her on Twitter under
the handle @LuDaRosaBooks.

Also by Luana DaRosa

Falling for Her Off-Limits Boss
Her Secret Rio Baby

Discover more at millsandboon.co.uk.

FALLING AGAIN FOR THE BRAZILIAN DOC

LUANA DaROSA

MILLS & BOON

First published in Great Britain 2023
by Mills & Boon, an imprint of HarperCollins*Publishers* Ltd,
1 London Bridge Street, London, SE1 9GF

www.harpercollins.co.uk

HarperCollins*Publishers*
Macken House, 39/40 Mayor Street Upper,
Dublin 1, D01 C9W8, Ireland

Large Print edition 2023

Falling Again for the Brazilian Doc © 2023 Luana DaRosa

ISBN: 978-0-263-29732-4

07/23

For Velo. I love you.

For which I love you

CHAPTER ONE

THE MOST UNUSUAL sensation had pooled inside Yara since she had stepped over the threshold of the hospital. Like a fiery liquid, it surrounded her stomach and filled her chest with every breath. It took a while for her to realise what that sensation was—*nerves*. For the first time in what felt like an eternity, Yara felt nervous.

Salvador.

Her heart pounded against her chest as she thought of the man she hadn't seen in thirty years. Once they'd been inseparable—now she didn't even know what he looked like or what had happened in the three decades since she left Brasília. It was by pure chance that she knew he worked at Centro Médico Juliana Amala, the hospital that had hired her to consult on a difficult case.

Salvador Martins.

Yara shifted in the chair she sat in, picking up the glass of water they had put in front of her without taking a sip. Her fingers traced along the condensation on the outside of the glass, picking up the tiny pearls of water until her fingertips were slick. She quickly put the glass back down, not trusting herself with such a fragile object.

What on earth was wrong with her? Yara had spent the years since becoming a doctor making a name for herself as a top general surgeon and a sharp-minded diagnostician whom other doctors turned to when they were at the end of their rope with the diagnosis of a patient.

Yara was at the Juliana Amala because she needed to help a team of doctors find out what was wrong with their patient. She should not be nervous—she wouldn't be, were it not for Salvador and the host of ancient feelings his memory resurrected from the deep and dusty corners of her mind. Would he have realised it was her coming to consult on the case? Was he as nervous to see her as she was to see him?

With the way she had left things with him, she doubted that. Their friendship had blossomed into something more serious when she had left for med school in Porto Alegre, far to the south of Brasília, her hometown. During her teenage years her parents had voiced their displeasure at the kind of company she chose to keep. When it came to Salvador, they hadn't held back with their negative opinions, letting her know that, as their eldest daughter, she was expected to enter into a good marriage with a man from a good family that would be worthy of the Lopes name. Someone like Lawrence Silvia—the son of family friends, and her ex-husband of one year.

They had begun to pressure her when they realised that they couldn't dissuade her from being with Salvador, dangling the one thing in front of her they knew she couldn't refuse—her tuition for medical school. Without their financial help her dream of becoming a doctor would have ended right there, along with the approval she so desperately craved from her parents.

And for what? Once Yara had left her childhood home for good, neither of them had cared much what was going on in her life. Was their only motivation to push her so hard in one direction so they could brag to their friends about it? Only for them to realise that nobody cared about this.

By the time her sister, Bianca, was old enough

to choose a path for herself, their strange obsession with status had shifted. Or had they been easier on her because she was a surprise child?

Yara didn't know, and she didn't care enough to find out any more. Though the memory still burned in her chest, she had realised long ago that she needed to make her own peace with it.

The door opened, pulling her out of her pain-filled memories, and a man she'd met in several video calls strode in with a laptop under his arm. He came to a halt in front of her, stretching his hand out.

Yara got up, quickly wiping her wet fingers on the side of her skirt before she grabbed the hand in a strong shake.

'Hello, Dr Sakamoto, it's a pleasure to meet you in person,' she greeted the Chief of Medicine of the hospital.

'Likewise, Dr Silvia. I'm glad to have you here. The team and I can't wait to get started on this,' he replied and handed the laptop to her as he let go of her hand. 'These are all the patient scans, files, exams and test results we have on Mr Orlay. The entire team is on standby. If you have any questions, just give them a page.'

He nodded his chin at the phone line on the

desk. 'We turned this small conference room into your office for the duration of your stay.'

Yara smiled. 'Thank you.' She nodded as she looked around. With any luck, she wouldn't be spending too much time in this room, but rather talking to the different doctors about their theories on the patient.

As she had prepared to come to Brasília, she had asked for daily updates on the patient. Her last case had ended almost two days ago, but flying in from Singapore meant Yara had to make the choice between sleeping or reading up on the case—and she could never sleep knowing it would leave her underprepared.

Mr Orlay had come into the hospital for a procedure on his heart that he had never fully recovered from. From the briefing material Dr Sakamoto had sent, she could see that the team here had already gone through some neurological tests, yielding a lot of different results that didn't make any sense to them.

'I'd like to see the patient before I look at his file. I need to do my own exam so I can check for any inaccuracies or potentially false conclusions.' This was usually the part where she noticed some resistance from the doctors she worked with on different cases. No one liked the outsider to come into their space, telling them they were wrong about a step in the diagnosis—even though if they weren't, she wouldn't be here.

A feeling Yara understood well. She hadn't come as far as she had without learning from her mistakes. Though her parents' unending pressure for perfection had almost broken her at times, the resilience she had to establish to withstand the expectations during her younger adult years helped her to this day when it came to her career.

Dr Sakamoto, however, took the comment without even flinching, leading her outside the office and down the corridor, where they came to a halt in front of a closed door. 'We chose that conference room due to its proximity to the patient room,' he said when he noticed Yara's gaze flicking backwards.

They were in the general wing of the medical centre, in what Yara believed to be a more secluded area. Both the floors and the walls shone at her in a soothing off-white. The absence of scuffs and marks that she often saw in other hospitals showed her the age of the *centro médico*. If she had to guess, she would say the Juliana Amala had been founded no more than five years ago. That or Chief Sakamoto had run a renovation crew through just to impress her.

And Yara definitely was impressed. This was by far one of the nicest hospitals she had been to, the space light and airy rather than functional, giving patients a relaxing environment so they could focus on healing and recovery.

The doors along the corridor they walked down were spaced out, with each bearing a name on the frosted glass panes. Someone had probably had to vacate their office to turn it into a patient room for the duration of her stay here.

A detail that made her smirk on the inside. Some hospital administrators couldn't resist the urge to impress her with strange fanfares such as this one. She appreciated the convenience, but her main focus would always be the patient, and it didn't matter how far she had to walk for that.

The Chief of Medicine knocked and opened the door a second later, leading her into the patient room.

A man in his sixties lay in the bed in front

of her, the heavy bags under his eyes and the washed-out complexion hinting at the strain this mystery disease had on him.

'*Bom dia, senhor.* I'm Dr Silvia and I'm here to assist the team with your diagnosis. Are you okay with me examining you?'

'*Sim.*' His voice was raspy, no doubt from the breathing tube they had him on as he recovered from his surgery.

Yara turned to the patient and grabbed her stethoscope to listen to the patient's chest. Breath signs were shallow but there. Enough to breathe on his own—for now. According to the brief she'd received when she agreed to consult on this case, Mr Orlay had been suffering from an unexplained and progressive weakness ever since he woke up from surgery.

Listening to his heart, she could tell that his new valve was moving enough blood to keep him alive, yet he didn't have enough energy to even get out of bed to do his post-surgical physiotherapy.

Had it been something between the surgery and now that had put him in such a state? Medication they'd given him as prophylaxis? Or was this an unknown disease digging its claws deeper with each passing minute, unaffected by any treatment they tried? Something unrelated to his previously weakened heart valve?

Yara made a mental note to check the list of medication he was on and to stop anything that wasn't warranted by the symptoms she could see. Then she took a small pen-light out of her pocket, testing his pupillary reaction—normal. No sign of any neurological damage.

'Thank you, Mr Orlay. I'm hoping to get to the bottom of this. I'll be back shortly to discuss our next course of action.'

This was much better. The moment the Chief of Medicine had walked in with the information package around the patient, Yara had felt back in control and on an even keel. Diagnosing patients—that was what she needed to concern herself with. Not her girlhood boyfriend and what their reunion would be like.

With a critical patient at hand, she didn't have time to devote herself to any kind of lengthy catch-up, anyway. Her primary focus would be solving this medical mystery and then she would leave her home city behind again.

Maybe she was making too much of it in her mind. Three decades had passed since they had seen each other and, while Yara had never tried to get in touch with him over the years, neither had he. So maybe he didn't want to see her, and their brief reunion would be all about the medicine and nothing else.

Maybe it was better this way.

Salvador closed his eyes for a moment, letting the deep sigh building in his chest escape into the room. In front of him were the scans of Henrique Orlay, a patient suffering from a strange post-surgical side-effect no one could make anything of. He himself had spent the last four days scrutinising the patient's scans, looking them over with a literal magnifying glass, turning them this way and that way in an attempt to find something—anything—to help this man who seemed to struggle to hold on to life for no particular reason.

Things had turned so dire that Chief Sakamoto had brought in some famous consultant to advise them on this case. His colleagues working on the case with him had bristled at the suggestion that they were no longer deemed good enough to solve this on their own, but Salvador cared little.

LUANA DaROSA 17

All he wanted to do was a good job—for his own sake and the sake of his nephew, who had recently come to live with him full-time. The hours were already tough, and having a critical patient only made things worse. Since he'd been the one with the patient from the very beginning, he was the radiologist most involved in the case. Other people on his team could run the scans, but he'd been the one studying them all in such detail. If anyone would spot anything, it'd be him.

His phone lit up, and he looked at it, reading the reminder he had set for himself. Chief Sakamoto wanted an updated contrast MRI, but when Salvador had arrived at the patient's room earlier, the man had still been sleeping. By now, the trainee doctors and med students would have done their rounds, and he'd be able to transport the patient.

When he got to the patient's room, he found the door slightly ajar and spotted the familiar figure of Chief Sakamoto in the room, along with someone else, who had to be the consulting doctor to help them figure out the case.

Salvador stopped in the doorway, his eyes drawn to the woman. She wasn't wearing anything remarkable—a dark blue blouse and a pencil skirt—yet his reaction to her was as instant as it was unexpected. His eyes followed the gentle curve of her neck as she leaned forward to listen to the patient's heartbeat. A few strands of her dark brown hair had fought themselves out of the grip of the hair tie holding the rest of her locks in a bun at her nape.

Her lips were drawn down slightly—because of the situation with the patient, or had something else displeased her? Whatever it was, Salvador's gaze lingered on them, their shape suggesting unending softness and...and what?

He blinked, trying to rid himself of the sudden fantasy coming over him and forced his attention back into the room. What was her name again? Salvador had received the news of the doctor joining them a couple of days ago, along with the rest of the team assigned to Mr Orlay's case.

He couldn't remember her last name, though he knew her first name, as that name was permanently branded into a hidden part of his soul. *Yara*.

Even after all these years, the thought of his teenage sweetheart came with a strange sense of melancholy—as if he had lost a piece of himself when she left this city, and him, saying goodbye for the last time without his knowing it was a final farewell. The confusion and hurt had lessened over the three decades that had passed since he last saw her, but remnants of their time together still remained within him. Or rather, the betrayal he'd experienced had taught him to never let his guard down with anyone. No matter how much he *believed* he knew someone, in the end he had to remember that people changed. They did whatever was best for them and nobody else.

Just like Yara had done. Something he actually owed her a debt of gratitude for. If she hadn't cut him out of her life the way she had, he'd still chase the belief that he was worthy of more than what life currently had to offer. Thanks to her, Salvador had been able to keep his relationships casual, never letting anyone get too attached to him.

His most recent ex, Edinho, had come close to breaking through the heavy fortification he'd built around his heart. But even he had failed when it came to the ultimate test—Salvador's duty towards his nephew. Keeping Felix safe and out of trouble was the one calling that made Salvador feel worthy of his place in society.

'Ah, Martins, good of you to join us so I can introduce you to Dr Silvia.' Chief Sakamoto had spotted him, ripping him out of his contemplations over the scars dwelling beneath the surface.

Salvador's eyes drifted back to Dr Silvia, who was still facing the patient, and he watched with bewilderment as her entire posture stiffened. The gentle look on her half-obscured face melted away, into an expression he wasn't able to understand from this angle.

Surprise? Wasn't she expecting to meet the doctors on her team?

'It's nice to meet you, Dr Silvia. I'm Salvador Martins, your radiologist on the case.' He stepped forward to stretch out his hand but stopped cold when a familiar sensation washed over him.

Dr Silvia hesitated for a moment, and when she finally turned around, the ghost of something ancient came rushing at him, a sense of familiarity that was impossible. It felt as though a connection fell back into place—back where it belonged—and the sheer force of it pressed the air out of his lungs.

She looked at him, her light brown eyes wide, darting all over his body for a moment before they settled on his face.

This feeling… It couldn't be right. How?

'Yara?' He forced the name over his lips, praying that he might be mistaken. Or that he might be right. The emotions were such a whirl within his chest, he didn't know how he *wanted* to feel.

The woman in front of him gave a nod, as if she understood he needed a sign to tell him she was really her.

'Hello, Salvador,' she said, her voice coated in something he couldn't decipher.

'You two already know each other?' Chief Sakamoto looked at him with a playfully hurt expression, as if he was angry he hadn't told him.

'I didn't know you were Dr Silvia,' he said, fighting through the fog that had come over his brain. 'You changed your name.'

A quick expression fluttered over her face, something painful that she shoved away just as fast as it had appeared. 'People tend to do that when they get married.'

'They do. But you said you wouldn't.' The words came out of his mouth before Salvador could understand where they had even come from. This conversation he was recalling had happened when they were teenagers, fickle beings whose words were worth little to their adult selves.

Only Yara had been so adamant about it. Her family name had been part of her. *Lopes*. It was strange to believe she had changed her mind. Then again, the woman in front of him wasn't the girl he had used to know.

He'd do well to remember that.

Yara opened her mouth in a response that wouldn't come, for her brain had been wiped clear of any thought the second her eyes had met Salvador's in a moment that had been in the making for decades.

And in all the years she'd thought about what their reunion would be like, she'd never thought it would be *those* words he hurled at her, aiming for a weakness he couldn't know lay bare underneath her skin.

What was she supposed to say to that? That her parents had believed him beneath her, so they pressured her into marriage to a different man? One that had stripped all meaning from the name Yara Lopes to the point where she didn't know if that woman still existed? If that was who Salvador wanted to meet, it would be better for him to find out now that *his* Yara was long gone.

No one knew about her divorce or how broken it had left her. She certainly wasn't going to break her silence for Salvador. There were a lot of things she owed him, but that part of her story wasn't one. What had happened with Lawrence was one of the reasons she had avoided coming back to Brazil, choosing instead to travel the world and make a career out of it. No one could ask questions if she never spent more than a week in one place, and she could keep her secret to herself for just a bit longer.

How could she admit that her parents had wielded so much power over her, threatening her future and her dream if she didn't do as they asked? She had believed them to have her best interests in mind, despite their stooping low to force her hand. And instead of fighting for Salvador, the man her younger self had believed could be the one, she gave in to the pressure, scared to lose her spot at the University of Rio Grande do Sul if she didn't comply with their orders.

'I'm originally from Brasília,' she said towards Dr Sakamoto, who shot puzzled looks between them. 'We went to school together.'

He nodded, seemingly satisfied with her explanation, and turned his attention to Salvador.

'Ah, in this case, I trust you will take some time to get your old friend acquainted with the hospital? Introduce her to everyone in the team?'

Salvador nodded, his spine so stiff from the surprise he looked almost menacing as he towered over the already tall Dr Sakamoto. The Chief only smiled, either unaware of the tension between them or choosing to ignore it altogether, as he nodded to both of them and left.

Silence filled the room, only interrupted by the soft whirring and beeping of the monitor Mr Orlay was hooked up to. There were so many things she wanted to say to him, yet none of the words formed in her head.

How did one apologise for ghosting their teenage boyfriend thirty years after the fact?

'Can we have a word outside?' A different setting was definitely the first step.

Salvador glanced at her for a second before moving to the patient. 'Henrique, I'm afraid we have to take you for another ride to the MRI. You're still familiar with this?' He pulled gloves over his hands before showing him a syringe filled with a dark liquid.

Mr Orlay nodded with a sigh that showed just how much he'd already been probed and prodded as they tried to cure him from his mystery ailment. Yara hoped she didn't have to add too many procedures to his time here before she found out what ailed him.

Salvador had picked up on his unease as well, for he pulled up a stool for a moment so they could be at eye level with each other. 'I've got good news for you, Henry. We flew this kick-ass doctor in to treat you. If anyone can find out what's going on, it'll be her. You just have to hang in there a little longer.'

Yara wasn't sure if some colour had returned to Mr Orlay's face or if she just imagined it, but she was surprised when he managed to smile at Salvador with a tired nod.

'I'll inject the contrast agent now and then we'll take you down for the scan.' He got off the chair and injected the agent through the cannula in his hand. 'Let me arrange an escort for you and I'll see you in a moment.'

Yara had watched the entire interaction with a warm feeling pooling in the pit of her stomach, which slowly spread through her entire body. She was glad to see that the years had not robbed him of his kindness. He'd always been a caring person, looking out for the weaker people around him and helping them stand strong. Qualities she had always admired in him. It was what had once driven her to strive to be better.

She unfroze when Salvador passed her with barely more than a glance, walking out of the room and down the corridor to the nurses' station, where he ordered the MRI for Mr Orlay.

'Salvador,' she called when she caught up with him and fell silent when he turned around to face her, his eyes filled with an ancient pain she hadn't expected.

'I can't talk right now, Yara, and I'm not even

sure I want to,' he said when the nurse had stepped away and they were alone for the first time.

'I just need one minute. For better or for worse, we'll be working together on this for the next few days. So, I want to take a moment to…clear the air. I know nothing I can say will make a difference, but at least give me the chance to listen to you and just…take it.'

She didn't want to insult him with empty apologies that rang hollow with the decades they had been left unsaid.

Salvador crossed his arms in front of his chest, his jaw rolling as he considered her words, and with each passing second the knot in her stomach got tighter.

This was so not how she had imagined any of this would go. Sure, she knew he was going to be angry. He had every right to be. But, knowing the kind soul beneath the gruff exterior, she also truly had thought he'd give her a chance to say what she had to say. If, at the end of that, he decided that the hurt ran too deep, Yara would let it be and work with him in any professional capacity necessary.

Though as she watched Salvador silently

making the decision of whether he wanted to hear her out, she realised that not a small part of her wanted to reconcile with him. Their friendship had meant so much to her and if it hadn't been for the pressure her parents put on her they might have seen their budding romance come to fruition. Her heart had called for him even as she decided to leave, choosing her dream of becoming a physician over their relationship—just as her parents had wanted her to.

'I can't deal with this right now, Yara,' Salvador finally said, and those words cracked her chest open. Disappointment flooded her system, extinguishing the tiny glimmer of hope she had nurtured on her way here.

His gaze flickered over her shoulder and she followed it, watching as someone from their medical team wheeled Mr Orlay down the corridor.

'It doesn't have to be much. Just one cup of coffee in between patients. We'll be working together on this, no matter how we feel about each other—so I need to know there won't be any problems.'

She was the lead physician on this case, after

all, and there was truth in her reasoning. They *were* going to work together, and the tension between them wouldn't help with the patient's care, especially not if either of them was constantly thinking about the other one.

'Give me one minute of your time, Salvador,' she said when his eyes drifted back to her, his glare hard and unreadable.

The line of his jaw tightened as his chest rose in a deep inhale. 'I'm needed for the scan.'

CHAPTER TWO

THE SERENITY OF the hospital was broken and Salvador knew exactly who to blame. Though the department was always buzzing and hectic, this was the place he could feel in control and at peace with himself. Here he was the master of his own fate, working with a team of physicians as passionate and dedicated as him.

It was where he could do the most good—outside of taking care of his nephew and giving him the life he deserved. A life Salvador had had to build for himself. His parents had failed both him and his brother with their problematic life choices, going so far as to drag Felipe down with them. Salvador didn't know how he'd scraped by without any lasting damage.

Yara. Memories of her popped into his mind unbidden. She'd often invited him to her home after school, letting him stay over whenever she sensed something off around him. Those had been the days his parents had fought over debt and money, their ire so uncontrollable that their children often became collateral damage.

And she'd never asked for an explanation of what happened, just accepting him into her home and her heart without the judgement he experienced from other people from her socio-economic background—or at least so he thought, until she had left him without a single word. He'd spent so many years wondering why, unable to move on from that intense heartache. Their romance had just begun when she left to attend medical school, but the anger and pain had been enough to dissuade him from anything serious over the years since then. If he never again felt the way he did when Yara left, his life would be much simpler and free of hurt.

Though despite the anger simmering underneath his skin, he had to admit that she'd saved his life, and she didn't even know about it. The sanctuary of her home had given him the emotional distance he had needed not to fall into the same patterns of bad behaviour his parents had perpetuated. He owed her gratitude beyond any measure that he could ever hope to repay—and yet it was pain that pumped through his veins whenever he caught a memory of her drifting through his head.

Or was the heat he felt something else? The last remnant of a dying ember that had been the whirlwind of their budding relationship? No, that couldn't be it. Their attraction to each other had only *just* emerged when Yara had left for Porto Alegre. The number of kisses they had shared could be counted on one hand. Her abrupt actions had put a stop to much else, but those precious few weeks had been enough to make him dream about a future.

Salvador pushed it all away as the door next to him opened. A junior radiologist stepped in, holding a tablet. 'Here are the scans, Dr Martins,' he said as he held out his hands.

He grabbed the tablet with a nod of thanks, glancing at the scans for a moment before turning it off and tucking it under his arm. After Mr Orlay's scan, Salvador had received two additional requests to handle. Those were the more complex cases in the hospital, where they had already gone through several rounds of different scans.

The one the radiologist had handed him was

a new case, but none the less a tricky one. The symptoms of the patient were disjointed, none of them pointing in a more concrete direction— so the physician on the case had requested Salvador to walk him through the scans.

'Is Dr Douglas going to see the patient now?' he asked, hoping he'd know the answer.

But his colleague shook his head. 'He's asked us to transport her back to her room, and he would see her after his next consultation.'

Salvador nodded and pushed himself off his chair. 'I'll ask the nurses' station to page him.'

The charge nurse informed him that Dr Douglas was running a training lab with the medical students and would be able to look at the scans after the class in the afternoon. Salvador glanced at his phone, checking the time.

Part of him wanted to be too busy to indulge Yara's request for a short meeting. She wanted to speak about what had happened between them all those years ago—a conversation he'd long since lost hope would ever happen. He'd been forced to make his peace with it, not knowing what drove her away or what they could have been had they stayed.

Would they have been happy? He hadn't known who he was when they first met, only realising much later that he was both attracted to women and men. How would his sexual exploration have turned out if he had tied himself to a woman for ever at such a young age?

Or were these just convenient excuses that he clung on to because he didn't believe that he could have made someone like Yara, who had known nothing but safety and splendour, happy? When his life was streaked with the discord and chaos crime and poverty brought to anyone who came in contact with it? He remembered both the glares and the whispers following him as they walked around in her neighbourhood, unworthy to even touch her the way he desired.

But Yara was right. Like it or not, they had to work on this patient as part of a team. That meant no distractions or tension that could lead to mistakes.

Biting back a sigh, he headed for the general medicine wing, where Yara had her office. On a whim, he stopped when he passed one of the staff rooms and grabbed two packets of crisps from a vending machine before knocking on the door of Yara's temporary office.

'Come in.' Her voice sounded through the door.

Yara was staring at her laptop with narrowed eyes, the fingers of her right hand twirling a pen. The notepad next to her was already filled with annotations in a tiny script.

An involuntary smile spread over Salvador's face. He had used to make fun of her for her tiny handwriting, making her notes at school so much harder to read—and she'd been a lot more diligent about her notes than him.

'I'd offer to go over your patient notes with you, but I forgot my magnifying glass at home,' he jested before he could stop himself.

Yara's head whipped towards him, eyes wide with surprise. Being off in her own world was just like her as well.

'Salvador... Hey.'

His eyes darted to her throat when it bobbed slightly. Had she been waiting for someone else? The discomfort in her stance was apparent, and he couldn't blame her. After thirty years, he'd not thought they would reunite—or be in the position where they had to lay open the things that had happened between them. That moment in their youth when they had both realised there was more between them, followed by Yara drifting out of his life without an explanation.

Salvador wasn't sure he even wanted to know any more.

'I have a minute if you want to chat,' he forced himself to say, taking a step in and closing the door behind him.

'Sure...' There was a slight hesitation in her voice before she continued. 'Please, have a seat.'

He sat down and handed one of the crisp packets to her. 'I thought all the dry patient notes might have left you with a small appetite.'

Yara picked up the crisps and turned the packet, with its bright green crocodile, around in her hand. 'Cheese flavoured?'

'You don't like them any more?' Salvador raised an eyebrow, a frown pulling on his lips.

'No, I do like them even though I know I shouldn't.' She smirked, her eyes scanning the list of ingredients. 'They're cheese flavoured, but real cheese has never touched them.'

She paused for a moment before opening

them. 'I can't believe you still remember what flavour I like. Or that I like these at all.' The snack was mostly marketed for children.

Salvador looked at the packet in his own hands for a moment. He hadn't *exactly* remembered. But rather, once he stood in front of the vending machine his hands had acted before he could even make a conscious decision, punching in the number to get this specific flavour and brand.

'How is your research going?' He didn't know what to say about the snack, so he changed the topic. How could he explain that he remembered something like that after three decades without sounding as though he still cared enough to do so?

'Good, I think. A very interesting medical puzzle. His heart surgery has thrown off a lot of the diagnosis, looking for a link where there isn't one.' She popped a crisp into her mouth, chewing for a moment. Her eyes went wide as she looked at him. 'How do these things still taste the same?'

He smiled, opening his own packet and trying one of them. The taste of artificial cheese exploded in his mouth. 'I don't know how you like these,' he mumbled.

Yara laughed, the sound of it bringing memories of a time they had done nothing but laugh with each other. They sprang to life in his head, settling heavily in the pit of his stomach.

'It's comfort food. It doesn't have to taste nice,' she said, with a smile that looked exactly as he remembered.

His gaze drifted up and down her face as he took the time to look at her in the quiet of the moment they shared. She hadn't changed much over the years, the light brown hue of her eyes still dotted with the occasional black mark and shining with the curiosity that had always lived in them. Once he'd look into those eyes and young, evolving love would threaten to constrict his chest. Now he saw her and the hurt and anger he believed to have moved on from ages ago came bubbling back to the surface.

'Are those the high-contrast scans?' Yara asked, nodding at the tablet he'd put on the desk when he sat down.

'No, this is a different patient—she's only arrived this morning from a different hospital.'

'Can I see them?' The curiosity he'd remembered only moments ago came to life in her eyes as he unlocked the tablet and brought up the scans.

'Unexplained weight loss and tiredness brought her here through a referral after her local hospital ran out of diagnostic options.' Salvador provided the context as she zoomed in on the scans.

Yara stayed quiet for a few heartbeats, tilting her head to one side while her fingers kept twirling the pen in her fingers, as if that helped her focus on the thing in front of her. 'Ah, interesting...' she mumbled.

'What is?'

She looked at him, handing the tablet back to him. 'Can you show me the patient chart? I need to know what the doctors observed outside of the two things you listed.'

'Are you trying to diagnose the patient?' Salvador raised an eyebrow at her. He'd looked at the scans already, noticing the inflammation around the aorta. But combined with the weight loss and tiredness, it could be one of many things. General medicine would have to narrow it down.

Surely she couldn't have already diagnosed her just by looking at a scan?

He took the tablet and brought up the patient chart, handing it back to Yara, who smiled at him with a grateful nod. Her eyes darted across the extensive notes from the patient's initial examination, as well as the transfer documents.

Yara remained quiet as she read. Until she finally breathed, 'Ah, she has vasculitis.'

'You can tell that from the scans?' Salvador didn't quite manage to keep the incredulity out of his voice.

'And from the notes.' She tipped on the tablet, highlighting what she had just read. 'She has a decreased pulse in her arm. Along with the tiredness and the inflammation visible on the scan, she has Takayasu Arteritis.'

Salvador furrowed his brow. 'I don't think the medical school I went to covered this disease in depth.'

'Oh...' Her lips parted as the tone escaped her throat, the expression of intrigue washed away. 'Pulseless Disease. You see, the pulmonary arteries here?' She indicated the scan. 'It's narrow around the inflammation. The notes mention a weak pulse in her left side—a common symptom when inflammation causes the arteries to swell and narrow.'

She paused for a moment, laughing softly. 'It's a fairly rare disease. I've only diagnosed it a handful of times. Lucky this came up when I was around.'

'Huh.' Salvador looked at the scans again before looking up at Yara as a strange sensation took root in his chest. They'd been sitting here for no more than a couple of minutes and she'd managed to diagnose a patient when an entire hospital had failed at it.

The girl he'd desired all those years ago had been ambitious, and it gave Salvador an unusual taste of satisfaction to see how far she'd come—mingled with the profound hurt that she'd chosen not to share this part of her life with him without giving him a chance to fight. No, she'd selfishly taken away any chance he might have had when she ignored all of his attempts to talk to her.

And why? Salvador hadn't believed that their difference in class had ever bothered her. She wasn't a person swayed by wealth or the perception of others. Even when gossips at school were passing comments about his father's criminal record, Yara had brushed it aside, seeing him for who he was—not for what his parents had done.

Until the day she'd abandoned him, and it became clear to him that he was unworthy and could never give her the kind of life she was used to. He'd stopped trying with anyone after that, leading a life of meaningless flings that never dipped below the surface. His latest relationship had started to look different, but even Ed had left when he realised that Salvador would never let his walls down. His kind and gentle nature had had Salvador almost convinced that he could have love in his life, after all. Until Ed had told him that he didn't want children right when Felix became his full-time ward.

Though maybe Yara's betrayal was something he could be grateful for, in a twisted way. What if his need to explore his attraction to men had got in the way of their relationship? When he'd first realised the feeling inside his chest when he looked at an attractive man was the same as he'd get from the women that he tied himself to for a night, he struggled to reconcile this attraction with the person he thought he was. It had taken many years and a lot of secret one-night stands before he understood that he was bisexual—and many more to understand that it was okay to be that way.

None of that would have happened if he had stayed with Yara, and how could he know that this wouldn't have caused them problems? Yet he still hurt, and he wanted to hear what she had to say about it.

'Why, Yara?'

Small fires started underneath her skin as Salvador's dark gaze drifted over her face and dipped below her neck, watching her with an unknown intent. Yara had been the one who wanted this conversation—had wanted it soon. Not because she particularly enjoyed going over her teenage insecurities, but she knew she needed harmony in this case if she wanted to do her job precisely and fast. She wanted to leave Brasília in under two weeks, to leave the city as soon as she could, before any of her family might realise that she was in town.

Yara hadn't made up her mind whether she wanted to pay her sister and cousins a visit or not. As much as she missed seeing them, she didn't want to talk about her marriage falling apart—didn't want to hear how she'd brought dishonour on her mother and all the terrible things her neighbours would whisper about her for having a divorced daughter. She wanted to avoid encountering the kind of pressure that had led her to the fatal decision of marrying someone because the match looked good on paper and would boost her family's reputation.

Though Yara was close to her sister, Bianca had never experienced the worst their parents had to offer. With almost ten years between the two women, their parents were a lot less concerned with what her sister wanted in life. After all, they had Yara to project all their unrealistic expectations onto.

Seeing the difference in treatment the sisters had received almost convinced Yara that their mother didn't know why she was like this herself. How could she be warm and understanding to Bianca while she settled all the pressure and anxiety of a fictitious reputation on Yara? Was that simply how her own mother—their grandmother—had modelled her life for her? Yara knew her mother was estranged from her own sister, and she had never actually met her aunt.

Or had her mother seen a lot more of herself

in Yara than in Bianca, forcing her to live a life that she could vicariously experience for her own satisfaction?

Whatever her reasons were, Yara had never found a conclusive answer, but she had to work hard to keep the resentment for her sister at bay. It wasn't Bianca's fault that they were treated differently.

As to why she had left... The reasons why she had decided to cut Salvador out of her life were shrouded in the years that had passed without her confronting the truth behind the extent of her parents' manipulation. How could she admit that they had threatened to take away the one thing she wanted more than anything else in her life when she wouldn't comply with their wishes?

And to make herself feel better about her choices, Yara had to believe that her parents simply meant the best for her when they pushed for a match with a man she hardly knew. What kind of parents would lead their child into a life of unhappiness for the sake of reputation? It took her many years to realise how much she'd been manipulated without noticing it.

The moment she had she filed for divorce

and left her marital home in the United States one year ago.

But those thoughts would remain unspoken for ever. She couldn't answer his question truthfully, not if that meant letting him see her scars.

'I was young and very stupid—though you probably already know that,' she said, cringing as she inched as close to the truth as she dared. She couldn't tell him everything, especially not what had happened since they drifted apart or how much she sometimes fantasised about how her life would look if they had had the chance to become a real couple.

'Look, if you don't want to tell me, don't. I gave up on the idea of closure many missed phone calls ago.' His voice rumbled deep, vibrating through the air between them and seeping into her skin as he crossed his arms.

His words found their mark as Yara bit her lip, taking it with the dignity she'd promised herself she would. Because he was right. After everything they shared with each other, she owed him more than *I'm sorry I ghosted you.*

Except the truth lay buried under an amount of insecurities and self-doubt she was unable to admit to anyone. She'd spent the year since her divorce finding herself again, and the process was so new and fragile, she didn't trust anyone near it.

'We've been friends for years and somewhere down the line the nature of our relationship changed,' Yara said, finding a way to get as close to the truth as she could. 'We became closer, and I thought it was what I wanted. But when I left, I realised maybe I didn't want to be more than friends—so I panicked.'

The lie tasted bitter in her mouth, but she forced her expression to stay neutral. She had panicked, but not because she had regrets— rather, she didn't know how to be so vulnerable in front of him, how to let him in by talking about the demands from her parents.

For their brief time together here in Brasília, it was better that he believed that rather than know the full truth about her insecurities.

She finally dared to look at Salvador again. His arms remained crossed on his chest, his eyes dark and narrowed as he scrutinised her.

There had been a time when he'd trusted her implicitly, never questioning or doubting her words. But that had been before she iced him out. Though it hurt, she could understand his hesitation. She still wasn't upfront with him about it, but she gave him as much as she could—and hoped that would be enough to restore civility between them.

'You didn't want to change our friendship?' He hesitated before he spoke those words, showing how much deliberation he put into his phrasing. Though his demeanour bordered on frosty, he still cared about her comfort—a realisation that thundered through her, leaving her tingling on the inside.

'I—I thought I knew what I wanted. But then I left for med school and panicked at the thought of coming back.' That at least was true, though for other reasons than Salvador now suspected. Her parents' relentless calls and pressure had worn Yara down, making her doubt her own ability to judge someone's character. Her mother had told her about the rumours surrounding Salvador's family, something she knew he struggled with, but she never asked and he never spoke about it, either.

He would have told her if he was in trouble, no? With all the doubt filling her heart, she didn't know any more. So instead, she'd avoided him—rarely a good strategy, but it was what she had gone with.

Silence spread between them. Salvador's eyes still lingered on her, peering deep into places Yara was sure he couldn't see. No one could see those.

Finally, he shook his head and breathed out a sigh. 'You could have said that,' he said, and the low rumble of his voice affected her deep inside, so much that she didn't quite manage to read his tone.

Was it relief that gave his voice such a soft quality? Had he blamed himself all these years?

'I'm sorry, Salvador. Back then, I was too self-involved to understand the gravity of my actions. But now I do, and I know it might not mean much now, but I always regretted losing you as my friend.' And that was the truth she needed him to know. Everything surrounding the break-up was still too personal for Yara to talk about, but she could tell him the truth that mattered—that she had missed having him in her life.

Salvador leaned back in his chair, his arms dropping to his sides, with a contemplative look on his face.

'I appreciate your apology, though I'm not sure I can or even want to be friends again. The way you left without a word almost broke me, and though I moved on, I remember the devastation I felt.'

His face was an unreadable mask as he spoke those words, their meaning cutting down to the bone. Even though she knew this to be the most likely outcome, her heart still squeezed inside her chest as the hope to have her friend back was extinguished by his icy stare.

'But I'm not going to cause any problems while we work together, as long as we keep our interactions related to the case,' he continued, at which point Yara nodded.

'That's all I really wanted to establish from this conversation.'

They were quiet again, but this time it was different. The previous tension that had filled the room didn't come back. Instead, a strange familiarity settled between them as they finally spoke about what happened thirty years ago.

'When are you going to see Bianca?' he asked.

'I don't know… It depends on how busy I am with this case and where I'm off to next. Work doesn't usually take me to Brazil, so it would be nice to spend some more time here, but I don't really get to decide when new cases come in.'

Salvador snorted, interrupting her rambling response. 'So you're avoiding your sister, too? Is there anyone in the city you're on good terms with?'

Yara's eyes went wide, and it took only a second to pick up on the playful notes in his voice. 'You're teasing me,' she said, crossing her arms. 'Is that what I should expect from you now for the rest of my stay here? You making fun of me until you feel better? That really doesn't seem related to the case.' She tried to give her voice a sanctimonious edge but couldn't help the relief shining through her words.

Teasing was good. Maybe that meant he'd changed his mind about being friendly, if not about being friends. Even though her apology was left intentionally vague, she did mean it, and a part of her wanted to find a way forward from the tension between them.

'I'm impressed with how fast you've diagnosed that patient. If you always work this quickly, we'll be done with Mr Orlay tomorrow morning,' Salvador said.

Though Yara knew exactly what kind of

value and expertise she brought to every hospital she visited, heat rushed to her cheeks at the compliment.

And then he smiled at her, and the flames that had been heating her face sent sparks flying all across her body, blazing fiery trails down her spine and exploding a tiny firework just behind her navel.

'Oh, with this patient I was just in the right place at the right time. While this is a rare disease, it is comparatively easy to diagnose. The difficulty lies in ruling out all the more common diseases before dusting off the medical encyclopaedias. The challenge with Mr Orlay is that so far his diagnosis has been made under the wrong impression.' The dark intensity in his gaze became too much for Yara. She dropped her eyes onto her notes, scanning over them.

She continued, 'His valve replacement led the diagnostic team onto the wrong path. He doesn't have one condition, he has two. A weakness of the heart that led to his valve replacement, and a pre-existing medical condition which explains the symptoms that cannot be explained with post-surgical complications.'

'You mean whatever ailed him was there before the surgery, but the symptoms matched his heart defect so we didn't think anything else was going on?' His expression turned thoughtful, and she watched with a hitch in her breath as his hand scrubbed over the stubbles on his cheeks.

He looked so different from the boy she'd fallen for, but beneath the years she still saw him.

'Yes, that's what I mean. Right now, I'm eliminating all the medication he's been put under because of the surgery. Once the drugs are out of his system, we—'

The chime of Salvador's phone interrupted her and he apologised. He looked at the display and got up. 'Dr Douglas is ready for me.' He picked up the tablet, tucking it under his arm. She held her breath as he passed, not wanting the ease they had finally found with each other to disappear again. Her stomach lurched when he stopped to look at her. 'We'll catch up later. Mr Orlay's condition has had the entire team working around the clock to get some results, so I'd like to hear more about your thoughts.'

'You know where to find me,' she said with

a chuckle that she hoped didn't sound as awkward to him as it did to her.

Her pulse pounded in her ears as she watched him walk away, a sight both strange and familiar. Age had only refined what had already been a handsome face, and for a moment she wished she could have seen it change over the years. Would she have spotted the subtle changes?

Yara shook those thoughts away, forcing them to the back of her mind. There would be plenty of opportunities to think about how their relationship could look like going forward.

Going by what she had seen today, he was still the same.

He was still her Salvador.

CHAPTER THREE

WHEN YARA ENTERED Mr Orlay's room, she found an unexpected guest sitting next to him. Salvador was wrapped up in a discussion with the patient, talking to him in a low voice. She couldn't understand the words spoken, but, from the cadence and the calm expression on his face, she surmised that they weren't talking about anything relating to his diagnosis. She cleared her throat to make both men aware of her presence. Salvador looked at her, and something mingling in his gaze immediately set her on edge.

Their conversation yesterday had shaken her, and the closure she yearned for was nowhere closer. He'd been distant whenever she saw him, giving her no more than a faint nod to acknowledge her.

The feeling of ancient desire still stirred through her, making it hard to think clearly. Her body remembered all too well what it felt like to lean against him, to breathe in his scent, to have his warmth seep into her. The ghosts of those memories kept creeping back into her mind, and they really needed to stop that. Any kind of romantic love they might have shared many years ago had died the moment Yara decided to put physical and emotional distance between them—a choice she'd come to regret with their unexpected reunion, but a choice she couldn't take back.

Judging by his own admission yesterday, he was not interested in her any more—be it as a friend or a lover. Not that she was hoping for any kind of reconciliation. No, she just wanted to do her job well. The sooner this was done, the earlier she would be able to leave Brazil.

'Good evening, Mr Orlay, Dr Martins. I'm doing my evening round before heading out and wanted to check on you.' She stepped closer to the bed and rested one hand at the foot of it, her eyes fully trained on the patient even though a tingling sensation in her nape urged her to look at Salvador.

'We discontinued most of your medication, leaving you only with the ones necessary to ensure your heart valve heals correctly. We've also kept you on some pain-management medication and have left instructions with the night nurse to increase your dosage. So if you are in any pain throughout the night, don't hesitate to tell the nurse.'

Mr Orlay nodded at her, the dark spots under his eyes saying enough of the kind of stress the diagnosis was putting him under. That alone was motivation enough to solve this case as soon as possible.

'*Obrigado,*' he said, his voice straining.

Yara gave him a reassuring smile. 'Of course. I'll see you in the morning.' Hopefully, whatever medication was counteracting further symptoms had left his system. She heard Salvador's whispers as she walked out of the room. The fine hairs along her neck stood on end as she sensed him following her out.

'Yara,' he called to her, and she stopped in her tracks, turning round.

He caught up with her, and the corners of his mouth twitched slightly upwards. That was his version of a smile. He had done that as a teenager as well, his lips only slightly twitching to indicate his amusement. He did smile, but those scarce full smiles were reserved for rare and treasured moments—such as when she had told him that she'd been accepted into her dream medical programme. They'd hugged and jumped up and down on the spot before he grabbed her by the shoulders and kissed her on an impulse. A kiss meant to be familial, but when their lips had come apart, both felt the world around them shift. Yara had shivered when Salvador's lips touched hers again, this kiss as charged and intimate as she had yearned it to be.

'Are you off now?' he asked, prompting Yara to furrow her brow. Not the question she'd been expecting.

'I'm done for the day, so just heading back to the hotel with some light reading for the evening.' She patted the tote bag full of medical journals she had picked up from the hospital's library.

Salvador paused, a hesitancy she couldn't quite place. His mouth opened, just to close again without his uttering a word.

'Can I drive you to the hotel? I imagine with all the travelling you don't have a car,' he finally said, and Yara got the strange impression that this hadn't been what he wanted to tell her.

Why was he offering to drive her? Was he looking for an excuse to spend time with her? The thought brought the relentless heat back into her veins, and she pushed it away. Nope, under no circumstances was she allowed to indulge those thoughts. Salvador was *not* interested in her in any way—couldn't be after she'd left him like that.

No, he was just being polite, for the sake of their professional relationship, as they worked on this case together.

'My hotel is just a short walk down the road. I booked it for its proximity to the hospital,' she said.

'Then let me walk with you. Just to be safe.' Genuine concern shone through his words, fanning the flames Yara had been trying her best to ignore.

These ancient feelings were getting way too out of hand. They had just managed to get into a place where they could be relatively comfortable with each other—after finally talking about what happened. Or rather, Yara had spoken while he had just taken it all in. This thought had followed her around all afternoon as she tried to focus on her work with the patient, poring through lab results and online databases in the hope that some missing piece of information would provide the context she was currently lacking.

Salvador hadn't actually said anything. He'd told her that she could have confided in him all these years ago and then…he'd changed the subject.

'Sure, if you think that's a good use of your time.' She tried to sound light-hearted, but her voice held a note of the uncertainty she'd been carrying around since their conversation earlier.

'Chief Sakamoto would be cross with me if I didn't make our VIP doctor feel welcome and taken care of,' he said, and as he walked back with her she felt his proximity with every step of the way, her body responding to an invisible pull as if he was a magnet and she no more than tiny pieces of metal—unable to resist.

'You're as dutiful as ever, Salvador,' she replied, and watched with satisfaction as the corners of his mouth twitched in the tell-tale sign of amusement.

They stepped outside the hospital together, and Yara took a deep breath as the warm air enveloped them. Summer was almost over, bringing the temperature down to a more bearable degree.

'I missed the heat,' she admitted as they started walking. 'I spend so much time in countries with a much more reserved climate, I don't get to enjoy the sun enough.'

'Right, you're one of those people that actually *enjoy* torturous heat.' He looked at her with raised eyebrows when she gasped at his words.

'I tell you, once you spend some time away from Brazil, you'll learn to appreciate the abundance of warmth and sunshine. I spent two months in London on a series of cases and I don't think I saw the sun once.' Her overdrawn dramatics had the desired effect when the corners of his lips twitched upwards, the hint of a smile lingering on his lips.

'Maybe one day I'll get to test that theory of yours.'

'Is your family still keeping you rooted here?' Yara had wanted to ask this question ever since he left her office earlier in the day—ever since she noticed that he hadn't shared anything in return.

The paranoid part of her brain worried he

might have caught on to her omissions, but how could he have? The things she kept to herself were the pieces of her life that would go with her into the afterlife—her parents' undue influence over her life, the demise of her marriage, how she *really* felt about Salvador years after she'd left Brasília.

None of these things had ever crossed her lips.

'In a sense. My parents passed away some years ago, at which point I stepped in to help Felipe and his girlfriend with their son.' He spoke slowly and deliberately, as if he put a lot of thought into the selection of his words—a caution that didn't surprise Yara.

His family had always been something difficult for him. His brother, Felipe, had used to get into a lot of trouble at school, leaving Salvador as the older sibling to deal with the fallout. Back then, Yara hadn't thought much of the things he needed to do for his family, thinking it was only right that he'd help them. After all, she understood duty to one's family more than anyone. It was that kind of obligation that drove her away from Salvador and into a marriage doomed from the start.

'Felipe had a child?' That was something she hadn't expected. Her mother had, on more than one occasion, called his brother a delinquent, and that image stood as a stark contrast to the one of a devoted father.

Salvador remained quiet for the next few steps, looking straight ahead with a blank expression. Finally, he nodded. 'His name is Felix. He's currently staying with me while Felipe…'

He left the sentence unfinished, and Yara didn't dare ask for more details. She'd only ever heard snippets of the lives of Salvador and his family when her sister called her, but she never engaged with the information too much. Talking about Salvador had the uncomfortable side-effect of bringing up ancient feelings that were wrapped up so tightly with her memories of him that she couldn't separate one from the other.

Why was he telling her that? Felix had been in and out of his care for almost all his life. Felipe had met his girlfriend at one of his usual dives, and it didn't take long to hear the news that they were having a child. The moment Salvador had heard of that, he'd started to worry about his unborn nephew. It had been a long time since Felipe had anything resembling a stable life and he was a frequent visitor in the local jail. Bringing a child into all that wasn't going to end well.

Salvador had once believed that his brother had pulled himself away from the bad crowd when he became a father, finding a legitimate job to keep his new family fed. But after their parents died ten years ago, he watched as Felipe fell back into his old habits, going into business with dangerous people—the same people that had landed his parents in that boat accident.

Meanwhile, Salvador had worked hard to lead an honest life and to shed the reputation and legacy of his family's name. Even though it hurt, he distanced himself from Felipe for his own mental health as well as to shield his reputation as a doctor.

Until his brother got himself into such trouble that his son came into the line of fire. For the sake of Felix, Salvador had let his brother back into his life, and sure enough it hadn't been long until the authorities had placed his nephew under his care.

Salvador was fiercely protective of Felix and

keeping him on the right path in life—so much that he didn't tell anyone about him outside of a handful of people he trusted implicitly. So why were these words pouring out of his mouth as if he couldn't help himself with Yara? Probably because he really couldn't. She'd been his confidant for so long, the information simply slipped out. He used to tell her everything, after all.

'This walk seems all right,' he said as they came to a stop in front of the hotel. 'I won't have to worry about you walking back and forth from the hospital on your own.'

Yara looked at him with an unreadable expression, her head slightly tipped to the side. 'You were worried about my safety?'

Her question took him by surprise. When he followed her out of Mr Orlay's room, he hadn't been quite sure why. She'd said that she was leaving, and all Salvador knew was that he really didn't want her to go just yet. He listened to her apology yesterday, a moment he'd been waiting for since she cut him out of her life without a single word. But instead of the closure he'd been expecting, it brought something else back to life within him—something dark and hungry that demanded to be fed. That something mingled with the resentment he still carried around, filling his veins with a fire that both enticed and devastated him.

Salvador realised that he had moved on from the pain, but he hadn't moved on from the *idea* of them. Despite the pain she had wrought on his life when she left after everything they had shared together, his flame for her had continued burning in a hidden corner of his heart.

A fire he had to put out straight away— though they might have been linked in a romantic sense thirty years ago, things were different now. She was Yara *Silvia* now. Married to someone else. The old affection stirring inside him had been inappropriate back then, but was even worse now as his target was a married woman.

A married woman he was still furious with.

'Of course,' he said despite himself. He could be accused of many things, but being a liar wasn't one of them. He had been worried about her, just as much as he didn't want to leave just yet. Something about her presence was… soothing.

'But since I have seen for myself that you'll

be fine on your own, I'll leave you to your evening.' His feelings for her were getting too loud in his head, and he needed to remove himself from the situation. They were inappropriate for a lot of reasons.

'You want to come in and have dinner?' Yara nodded towards the hotel entrance, and he narrowed his eyes for a second.

Dinner was the last thing he wanted with a married woman that had—within no more than a day and a half—coaxed his old affection for her out of him again. Except he really wanted to have dinner with her, despite the hurt and anger still burning in his veins. Was that part of moving on? Letting those sparks of raw emotion travel through his body when he was near her until they burned out? He struggled to understand the need for closeness bubbling up within him as it pushed against his desire to be left alone after all Yara had put him through.

Why was he interested in a dinner with this woman when she had left him so broken, he had never truly healed?

He glanced at his phone. 'I can't do dinner. I need to pick Felix up from practice soon.' Disappointment flickered over Yara's expression—

a sentiment he found mirrored in his own chest. 'How about a drink instead? I'd like to hear what you've been up to throughout the years.'

'Okay, let me just drop off my bag. I'll meet you at the bar?'

Salvador nodded and left the lobby to sit down at the bar, its dark wood gleaming in the dim light. Two weary patrons sat on one side, speaking in hushed tones, so he picked the chairs on the opposite side to sit down on.

Yara appeared a couple of minutes later, taking the seat next to him and sending a shock of awareness down his spine. Her proximity made him react, as it had when he'd first realised that his feelings for her had changed— that he wanted to be more to her.

Her smile was tentative, showing a hesitancy he noticed within himself as well. He'd been so shocked to see her yesterday. After three decades, he hadn't thought he'd ever see her again—or that all the affection he'd felt for her would roar back to life at the first sight of her.

'It's weird to be back,' Yara said as their beverages arrived. 'I thought about what would happen when I see you… Funny how reality always turns out to be so different.'

'You thought about meeting me again?' That possibility hadn't even crossed his mind, but it made sense. Had she known he worked at the hospital she was consulting with?

'Dr Sakamoto sent me the profiles of everyone on the team so I could see the people I'd be working with before I accepted,' she said, as if reading his thoughts.

'Ah, so you saw my name and knew a reunion was impending.' Yara had presented herself as a lot more collected than he had during their first meeting, and now he knew why. Though Salvador had to acknowledge that he had known her name, too. If he'd looked her up he would have recognised her instantly. He just hadn't cared enough about the consulting doctor to do so.

'Does your spouse travel with you?' he asked. Maybe if he heard her speak about her partner, he could create some additional distance. Nothing better to dampen the fire than the woman of his attention gushing about someone else.

But instead, Yara went rigid in her chair, her eyes trained on the glass of virgin caipirinha on the counter in front of her. He sensed her distress the second he'd said those words, and a moment later he understood why.

'No… I'm actually divorced.' And judging by her reaction, this must have ended in contention.

Not something Salvador had a lot of first-hand knowledge of. While his parents had led chaotic and volatile lives, they'd somehow stuck around. Though how good that had been for their personal development was questionable. Their bad habits and addictions had fuelled one another, leading to the accident that had ended up with both of them dead.

An eventuality Salvador had come to expect the moment he became old enough to understand what kind of self-destructive energy their marriage contained—and the darkness that was contained in the Martins DNA that he had fought so hard to escape.

'I'm sorry to hear that,' he said, not wanting to pry any further. Maybe the wound was still fresh.

'Thank you.'

Salvador watched as she took a sip from her drink, her manner calm and collected, but he still knew how to read beyond the exterior she wanted everyone to see—how her eyes were slightly widened, thoughts racing as she kept her composure intact.

'How has travelling the world been for you?' he asked, changing the subject.

Yara took another sip, her eyes closing for a moment longer than a blink would be, and when she looked back at him a smile lingered on her lips that tugged at a deeply buried place in his chest.

'It's been really great, actually. I get to see so many places around the world and meet so many talented medical professionals.' She chuckled, a genuine sound that vibrated through his skin and nestled itself into a deep part of his chest.

'Strange. You were more of a homebody back then. Even getting you out of the door for a quick walk proved to be an insurmountable challenge.' The memory bubbled to the surface unbidden, catching Salvador by surprise as he spoke.

The reason they had initially got to know each other was because of how far teenage Yara would go to avoid walking. Their physical education teacher had asked him to collect the exercise mats strewn around the gymnasium, and when he went to pick up the trolley he'd found Yara lying in it—reading a book. When he'd asked her what she was doing here she said she was waiting for someone to push the trolley closer to the door so she could finally leave.

The utter ridiculousness of her line of thought had immediately drawn him in, and they began hanging out in the gym after lessons. It was only when she invited him to her house that he realised how different their lives were—but by then his young heart had already grown too attached to her.

Salvador would have never taken her to be one to travel much.

'I…do it more out of necessity. Someone I used to work with asked me to consult on a case in New York. That was when I was still living in Seattle. We worked on a difficult case and from there they asked me to support them on a different case at a different location.' She paused, shrugging as she took another sip of her drink. 'And that's how I built a reputation.'

Her voice remained steady, but also somewhat detached, as though these were the words she'd practised many times over to deflect people from digging too deep.

Salvador was so close to asking the question she clearly didn't want to answer, but was interrupted when she laughed quietly while shaking her head. 'I don't know how I managed to talk myself into a career like that.'

A spark flickered to life where her laugh had made itself a nest inside his body, spreading a dangerous need with every beat of his ever-increasing pulse. His lips took on a life of their own, speaking the words forming in his mind before he could take a moment to think about them—to think about what being near this woman *still* meant to him.

She was divorced.

'I can understand why people pay you to advise them—because you're brilliant.'

Self-deprecation was a shield Yara had learned to wield with expert precision. What once had been a coping mechanism in a failing marriage had become so ingrained in her personality that she didn't even notice any more.

The teams she worked with valued her contribution and weren't shy of saying so—and in a professional setting, Yara found it easier to smile and accept.

But she couldn't recall the last time a man looked at her the way Salvador did right now, eyes narrow and full of a fire she couldn't name.

'That's very kind of you to say,' she said, a shiver running down her spine.

'Nothing kind about the truth.'

Her mouth went dry, and she was thankful for the choice of a non-alcoholic drink—for she took several large gulps to calm her nerves.

What was happening? Yara had invited him to dinner because…she hadn't wanted their conversation to end. It almost felt normal again, her partial confession yesterday helping to mend the fences between them.

In truth, she had believed Salvador would see the gaps she left blank and not believe her apology was genuine. But hearing about his nephew staying with him—maybe he understood better than anyone else that some demons were not allowed to ever see the surface.

Like the lead-up to and the eventual demise of her marriage—and the reason she'd jumped at the opportunity to be as far away from her former home in Seattle as possible.

Some things would stay hidden no matter

what. Or at least that was what Yara had thought.
Until he'd asked a question about her ex and
she'd replied with the truth.

Divorced.

Though early on she'd realised her marriage
wasn't going to be one to write epic romance
novels about, she never thought they'd end up
getting divorced... Or that it would be so difficult to admit it.

Yara hadn't got to where she was now because she gave up.

'I think I'll still thank you, just in case this
conversation somehow makes it back to my
mother.'

Salvador chuckled at the mention of her
mother. 'How is *Donna* Lopes? I won't even
ask if you'll go to see her.'

Despite the sensitive topic, Yara joined in
on the gentle laugh drawn from his throat at
the mention of her mother. Growing up, Salvador had had first-row seats to the whims
and demands the woman had put on her eldest
daughter, and had felt her disapproval almost
as much as Yara. The boy with parents of questionable integrity hadn't been good enough for
the Lopes family. Though her mother had never

said anything directly to him, her dislike of him had been barely veiled, and Yara would have been surprised if he hadn't picked up on it.

Hindsight made her trust in her mother's meddling look almost deranged. But whenever she went against her wishes, her mother's willingness to dangle the destruction of her dreams in front of her forced her back in line with ruthless efficiency.

'Well enough. You remember how much her interference agitates me, so I try to keep our conversations superficial,' she said.

'She used to get in your head.' He said it with gentleness, not with scorn as she'd expected. Without even trying—or knowing—he'd hit the root cause of their rift. Her parents had both meddled, pushing her in a direction she wasn't sure she should take. 'The insecure part of me sometimes wondered if you only put up with me because of how much it bothered both of your parents.'

Yara blinked at that comment. She'd never perceived him to be insecure in their friendship. Had she not been paying enough attention to him, too wrapped up in her own family drama?

'My parents didn't hold back with their hostility, I'll give you that,' she said as she looked back and remembered the scowls and thinly veiled comments launched in his direction. 'But when we met that day in the gym, my interest in you was genuine. Unfortunately, I did eventually listen to the poison they whispered in my ear. Something I regret, looking back.'

Salvador cocked his head to one side, an eyebrow slightly raised. The warmth radiating from his eyes enticed her to speak freely, the hint of his old affection for her lulling her into a sense of security as if he'd wrapped a cosy blanket around her.

'To be fair, I didn't quite understand what you saw in me, either,' he said, a self-deprecating chuckle tumbling from his lips.

'Are you kidding me? You moved the trolley over to the exit, so I didn't have to move one bit to get to my destination. That's when I knew you were someone I wanted to be friends with.' Their meeting had consisted of so much more than just that part, but she joined in with his humorous tone, and for a few heartbeats it almost seemed as though their old friendship could be salvaged, after all.

'You remember that moment?' he asked, prompting her to laugh at the absurdity of the question.

'Of course. How could I forget the moment I met you? At one point you were my best friend. I'll always cherish that memory, no matter what we might have become in the meantime.'

Yara cleared her throat as those words tumbled out of her mouth, struggling to shake the sense of nostalgic affection coming over her. Because what sparked to life in the pit of her stomach could only be described as nostalgia. There was no way any kind of *real* affection had survived the three decades they had spent apart. No, she was just yearning for lost years she couldn't have.

They were different people now, their lives no longer fitting together.

Salvador's expression turned soft for a moment, as if he, too, remembered the moment they spoke of, recalling the little details that had sparked such a deep friendship—and more. But then his face hardened, a dark presence taking over as she watched the walls around him thicken. The hint of their old connection she had sensed moments ago evaporated as if it had never existed.

'I'm glad we could talk, but I haven't changed my mind. We should keep things strictly professional, and I didn't mean to insinuate anything else by sitting down for a drink.'

His words hit with an unexpected ferocity that left her speechless for a few moments. 'That wasn't my intention. We've known each other for a long time and, while I'm not going out of my way seeking these conversations, it will happen as long as I'm here.' What was he expecting from her? That she would only ever say anything related to the case? Then he shouldn't have been the one to sit down with her in the first place.

'This is just...a lot. With everything I have going on, I just don't...' He left his sentence unfinished and glanced instead at his wrist. 'Sorry, I have to go,' he said when they both stayed quiet for far too long. He reached for his wallet, but Yara waved a hand.

'Don't worry about it. Go and get your nephew from practice. You don't want to be the parent who always shows up last, do you?'

Salvador laughed at the description of his parents. 'I can't believe you remember that small piece of information. These incidents have shaped my relationship with time in ways you can't imagine. If I'm on time, I'm already late.'

'I remember too well.' Yara joined in on the laugh, but quickly quieted. It was too easy to slip back into their old way of communicating with each other—especially when he had said he didn't want to.

Despite their banter, he reached for his wallet and took out some notes, which she swatted away. 'Seriously, go away! You bought lunch. It's only right I should get the drinks.'

Salvador crossed his arms, drawing her attention towards the lithe and impressive sight of him. Her breath caught in her throat, quickly prompting her to slide her eyes back up to his face before he could notice her checking him out. Going by the frown on his face, that effort had been in vain.

'Do you know how many packs of Yokitos I can buy for the amount on this bill?'

'Salvador, it's two drinks. You can stop being dramatic about it.' Yara sighed, rolling her eyes when his mouth formed a bemused line. 'How about I get this, and you get to the next one? Until one of us loses the game.'

'You're on, Lopes. And I'll tell you right now that I won't end up losing this.' Hearing her maiden name from his lips sent a shockwave through her body, hitting her with an unexpected ferocity that left her breathless for a second. She thankfully managed to swallow an audible gasp, not wanting to let anything on when she herself didn't understand this reaction.

Of course, he wouldn't call her Silvia. That wasn't how he'd known her.

'I look forward to the next round,' she said, hoping that she was imagining the tone of her voice that rang with a lot more longing than was appropriate. 'So we can talk about the case,' she added.

Salvador stopped and turned his head towards her again, and a glimpse of the softness she saw moments ago came back to his eyes. 'How about dinner at Pepe's tomorrow?'

Yara's eyebrows shot up at the mention of the familiar name. 'Pepe's diner still exists?'

'I don't think you could close that place even if you tried. The community just wouldn't allow it. They'd probably continue going there as if nothing had happened,' he said, only a slight twitch at the corner of his mouth indicating his amusement. 'Pepe retired some time ago. His stepson runs it now, but you'll see very little has changed. To you, it will probably look more like a museum than a diner.'

Dinner was probably a terrible idea, especially with the wellspring of old memories mingling with the attraction that had only intensified with age. Could she trust herself to keep things only relevant to their work?

'I...' He hesitated for a moment, looking at the wall behind the bar for a moment, seemingly looking for the right words. 'Despite everything, it was nice catching up with you, Yara. Maybe thirty years is enough time to hold a grudge, and we can start over. As two people who want to find out if they *maybe* can be friends.'

Yara stared at him, her grip around her glass tightening as her pulse accelerated. It should be comforting to know that the spark of friendship between them wasn't a figment of her imagination, but instead her blood heated with each pump of her heart, sending a searing heat coursing through her body.

At least there was nothing remotely romantic about Pepe's diner, and, though her blood ran hot inside her veins, she didn't want her own lack of sensibility to stand in the way of re-building some of the friendship they had shared for so many years. Maybe if she gave him some time, he could grow more comfortable in talking about their past.

And what was the harm if her feelings got a bit out of hand? The case would be wrapped up by next week, and Yara would be off to what-ever other team needed her help. There were several emails already waiting in her inbox.

'Okay, but only because I know you won't shut up about owing me something—your com-petitive spirit at its worst,' she said, her heart stuttering when his lips split into a full grin.

'See you tomorrow at seven, Lopes.' He raised his hand in a wave, and Yara summoned every ounce of willpower in her body to keep her eyes trained on the glass in front of her rather than trailing Salvador as he left.

She got up herself and made for her room,

with the strange sense stirring in her chest that she was walking into the lion's den with a smile on her face.

CHAPTER FOUR

'YOU GOOD?' SALVADOR sat down at the dining table and looked at his nephew, who was looking at his phone while piling the stew he'd made for him into his mouth.

Felix nodded, not interested enough to look up or to even answer him with anything more than a grunt. It had been like this for the last six months, ever since he'd come live with him, each conversation like pulling teeth.

Salvador bit back a sigh. He couldn't blame the boy. His life had always been in turmoil, culminating in his father's arrest, which led to the court appointing Salvador as Felix's legal guardian.

The doorbell rang and Salvador got up. Ciara, his neighbour's daughter, had agreed to watch Felix for a couple of hours. At twelve years old, he needed little supervision, but, given the fragile state Felix was still in, Salvador decided it would be better to have someone around.

'Thanks for coming over, Ciara,' he said as he let her in, grabbing his phone and keys off the side table. 'Take whatever you want from the fridge and call me if anything's up.'

She smiled at him. 'Sure thing, Salvador. Let me know if you're held up at the hospital. I can stick around.'

He froze for a moment, thinking about correcting her, but decided against it and closed the door behind him. Whenever he called her last-minute it was usually because of emergencies at the hospital. Had it been that long since he'd gone out to meet a friend?

Not that Yara was a friend. She was... Salvador didn't know how to finish that sentence. Once she had been the person he'd thought he would want to spend the rest of his life with. Though their romantic relationship had lasted less than a month, he'd been head over heels long before that. Now all these feelings came flooding back into his system, making it hard to see clearly.

He had wanted some closure, yes. But, damn him, he *still* wanted her. Thirty years and he was right back where they had been when she left Brasília to never return, never even call him either. Why was the affection he once felt for her roaring back to life within his chest as if she'd only been gone a day? The anger remained in the pit of his stomach, rearing its head whenever his mind drifted too far.

Though she had revealed some slivers of information he hadn't been aware of. While he knew her parents didn't approve of her choice of friend, he'd never thought she would be influenced by them. At the hospital Yara had said she panicked because she didn't want their relationship to change. But what if that was only part of the truth? Had she been pressured by her parents?

He wanted her back in his life. The strange invitation to dinner he'd extended showed him as much. But why did he want to be around her? To be friends? What could his damaged self even have to offer at this point? Even friendships went too deep for him, superficial flings being the only type of relationship he could manage. There was no trust involved in a fling.

She wasn't married any more.

Those words echoed in his mind, as if they were the only reason he had restrained himself—completely ignoring all the other reasons why heeding the pull coming from her was an overall terrible idea. He didn't even know how to be with someone like her, when he'd never been with anyone long-term. Edinho was the only serious relationship he'd had outside of Yara and look how that had turned out.

No, this dinner was only to talk about their patient and giving her any information he had that might aid the diagnosis. He would not let himself spiral out of control, keeping a tight grip on the erupting heat her eyes gliding over his body caused.

But his resolve was pierced with a sharp spear through his chest when he entered Pepe's diner and saw Yara sitting at a table near the entrance, her light brown eyes lighting up when she spotted him. A small smile curled his lips before he could fight it, and the smile he got in return almost knocked the wind out of his chest.

They stood in front of each other, neither sure what to expect from the other one as a greeting, until Yara stepped forward, giving him a hug that lasted less than two seconds before sitting back down. Her scent, however, lingered in the air—bergamot and something spicy he couldn't place. And beneath it, the smell of Yara, one that hadn't changed at all.

'Thanks for meeting me. I've already ordered—'

'The bread basket?' They said the word together, Yara's eyes widening as he spoke before her face relaxed into another smile that sent a trail of small sparks racing down his spine.

That was what they had used to share during long study sessions at Pepe's. Of course she still remembered. Why was he even surprised, when she had remembered so much else about their friendship?

'I got us our booth, too. Right next to Stanley.' She pointed at the replica of a sea creature that hung like a stuffed trophy on the wall next to them. No one they had ever asked had been able to accurately name whatever sea animal this trophy was supposed to be, looking simultaneously like a kraken and a starfish with its strange legs sticking out from a bulky head that had way too many eyes to be either.

'Stanley... That's a name I haven't heard in

a long time.' Yara had chosen it, saying that the three of them hung out so much that they should introduce themselves so he wouldn't betray all of the secrets he had been witness to.

For a few moments, they simply looked at each other, the ghost of what had used to be their deep friendship hanging between them, coalescing in this space where they had forged so many memories. Until Yara cleared her throat. 'How is Mr Orlay doing? Did you see anything on the new scans?'

Salvador shook his head. 'I was looking for lesions on his brain to confirm multiple sclerosis. Anything that would bring us closer to a diagnosis. But at least the nerve conduction velocity test we did on your orders yielded some results—though I'm not sure what they mean.'

Yara nodded. 'You were looking for multiple sclerosis? That makes sense. His patient notes say he had bilateral weakness in his legs after the surgery, which was written off as fatigue.'

'I think that was a fair call, given the man had just come out of a ventricular valve replacement.' Salvador crossed his hands in front of his chest, his defensive instincts kicking in.

Each one of his colleagues who had worked with Mr Orlay was on top of their game. He wouldn't let her tell anyone otherwise.

'Of course. Anyone would have thought this was because of his surgery. I'm here because we now know that it wasn't a side effect of his surgery. And since it isn't any type of MS, we needed to test the nerves along his arms to understand the severity of his weakness.' She paused for a second and the passion engulfing her eyes was a sight to behold.

Yara had looked like a pale ghost of herself when he arrived, the burden of what had happened between them lying heavy on her shoulders. The moment they spoke about their case, the Yara he'd known so well resurfaced, showing him the fire within her he hadn't been able to resist the second he'd first seen it. But he knew he had to, for his own sake. He was no longer the boy who'd fallen for Yara thirty years ago. Too much hurt had suffused their past relationship. How could he trust her when the pain still burned in his chest? Because it was *definitely* hurt that caused the heat to course through his veins.

'So all this time, we were following the wrong lead. He wasn't weak after his surgery...'

'But rather his surgery revealed a different condition,' Yara finished his thought, her hand diving into the bread basket that had appeared in front of them.

Salvador leaned back, once again impressed with her medical prowess. She had seen so much more than he could ever hope to see, and with the already growing heat inside him mingled a kernel of deep admiration of one medical professional for another.

'So, what's next for our patient?'

'I've stopped most of his medication. At this moment, I don't know what's a symptom and what's a side-effect from various medications running rampant through his system.' She frowned for a moment, waving the piece of bread in front of her face. 'He won't be comfortable, but it'll help us narrow down what's going on within his body. I asked the charge nurse to have someone page me if they see any drastic changes. But the NCV test narrows it down to a handful of potential diseases.'

Salvador settled back into his seat and was surprised when their main courses appeared in front of them. Had they been talking for so long already? The nervousness in his stomach had disappeared, leaving him with a sense of strange familiarity that he didn't know how to interpret.

They'd grown quiet for a moment but it was a different silence from the one they'd experienced in the hospital. This one was calm, easygoing, as if this brief interaction had somehow mended part of the thing she'd broken when she left Brasília—and Salvador.

Then his eyes narrowed slightly, his gaze turning dark for a moment, sending a shiver down her spine. She knew first-hand what a kind and generous heart beat within his chest—paired up with such looks, she had never stood a chance. Though those feelings were not real, she reminded herself. They were old feelings she had never resolved.

'How long has your nephew been staying with you?' she asked, to distract herself from the heat rising to her cheeks. Where was the cool composition she'd had a tight grip on only a couple of moments ago?

The dreamy spark in his eyes vanished within

a heartbeat, replaced by a cold gleam, and his lips thinned into a hard line that prompted Yara to hold her breath for a second. She'd stepped over a boundary she didn't know had existed. What had happened with Felipe that he had such a vehement reaction?

'He's been staying with me for half a year now. Before that, he'd been a long-term guest on and off for another year as my brother struggled to give him a stable home.' Some of his expression relaxed, and Yara let go of the breath she'd been holding.

'What about…?' She bit the inside of her cheek to stop herself from speaking any further. Something must have happened to his brother, or Salvador wouldn't have his nephew living with him.

'Felipe is in prison,' he said in a flat tone, and Yara struggled to comprehend his words for a few heartbeats.

'Prison?' An answer that shocked her even though she had half-expected it, knowing the rumours surrounding his family and upbringing. She recalled Felipe making questionable friends, and how often Salvador himself had sought refuge in her home—to the displeasure of her parents. Even before they had become more than friends, her parents had pushed the sons of their friends onto her in the hopes she would gain interest in someone they judged *better suited*. Another manipulation she had only been able to spot many years later.

Salvador nodded, his expression veiled and unreadable. 'He started to associate with some bad people during university and soon dropped out to take part in one of those friend's "businesses". I never asked what they were doing, but at one point the police picked them up. From then on it was a litany of minor offences which have put him in prison before for a couple of months. Something big was bound to happen. I was terrified of it, wanted to pull him out of this mess...'

The instinct to comfort him kicked in. She reached over the table and laid her hand on his forearm resting on the table. His skin was warm underneath her hand and the scent of soft lavender mixed with the smells of the food around them. The touch lasted for less than a few seconds before Yara realised what she had done and pulled her hand away as if she'd been burned.

What was wrong with her that she didn't have her impulses in check? Just yesterday they had spoken about keeping their connection professional, which didn't include comforting him over the table.

'Sorry, I didn't mean to—' she started, but he interrupted her with a shake of his head.

'It's…fine. You asked a question, and I answered it.' His voice was low and clipped, and the glimpse of vulnerability she'd spotted as he spoke about his brother disappeared into nonexistence. Only the heavy walls around him remained, imposing and impossible to overcome.

What had just happened? One moment she thought they might be able to restore some of their friendship again, only for him to slip further away from her. The comfort she sensed when they spoke about the past never lasted long, the shadow of her actions always looming over them.

She should just give up. They didn't have a chance, not with so much hurt between them.

Salvador was the first to break their intense stare, lowering his gaze as he reached for his drink. 'What about you? You said you don't want to visit Bianca?'

'I'm not sure. I might go to see my sister. But you know how nosy she is, and I'm not sure if I'm stable enough to withstand her overbearing nature.' Her sister and their network of cousins were a whole different challenge to Yara's stay here in Brazil. She hadn't told them she'd gone through a divorce.

Salvador raised one of his eyebrows. 'Why do you say that?'

'That's a very long and tiresome story,' Yara said, squirming under his gaze as his green eyes fixed on her.

'I…understand if you don't want to talk about it. After all, I was the one who didn't want to talk about these things.' Tension came rushing into the space between them, her breath catching in her throat for a moment before everything bled away just as fast as it had appeared.

A hint of the earlier vulnerability reappeared in his eyes, a sight so warm and enticing that the words formed in her throat before she could stop them.

'I got divorced, and I have told no one about it. It…wasn't pretty.' That was both an overstatement and an understatement of what had happened between her and Lawrence. 'It's been a year, but I just can't deal with it right now, and I know Bianca won't be able to resist the need to "fix it" when I just need some space to lick my wounds.'

To her surprise, Salvador only nodded, a solemn understanding in his eyes. 'Been in a similar situation when I became Felix's guardian. A twelve-year-old hadn't really been part of our plan together.'

'Really? Your wife left because you had to take in your nephew?' Who did such a thing, knowing the circumstances under which his nephew had come into his care?

'Ah, no, we weren't married. But yes, he left when it became clear that my brother wouldn't be released anytime soon, and Felix became my responsibility.'

The silence coming over Yara was deafening, and she blinked several times as her brain struggled to catch up with her jumbled thoughts. It was as if someone had turned off the volume on life for a second. *He?* The whirlwind the word caused inside her was disproportional to its length, forcing her own tangle of complicated feelings for Salvador into a new light she'd never even considered.

They had been seventeen when they gave in to the depth of emotion running between them, but that was three decades ago—a timeframe long enough for anyone to have their sexual awakening.

Was that why things seemed so uncomfortable between them? Not because of her actions, but rather that he'd never actually been interested in *her* as more than a friend?

The heat spreading under her skin at every intense look he shot her way turned into something confusing and disoriented as she tried to reconcile this information about him with the flood of old feelings infiltrating her system. Was she so bad at flirting that she couldn't distinguish a longing look from a neutral one?

'Wait…' She hesitated for a moment. How did one ask about this? 'You were—?'

The vibration of her phone rattled the table, interrupting her mid-sentence. She picked it up with an apologetic glance at Salvador and checked her notifications. 'It's the hospital. They're saying Mr Orlay is losing feeling in his legs and is now showing difficulties swallowing food.'

The message wiped the conversation they had

just had from her brain as she shifted her mind back into doctor mode, categorising the new symptoms into the plethora of other things she had observed around the patient and his condition.

Salvador nodded without hesitation and stood up. 'Put this on my tab, Baylor,' he shouted at the man behind the bar at the far end of the diner, who raised his hand to give him a thumbs-up. 'You ready?'

'Let's go.'

CHAPTER FIVE

THEY ARRIVED AT the hospital a few minutes later, heading straight for Mr Orlay's room. As they were walking, Salvador texted Ciara to let her know he'd indeed be stuck in the hospital for a bit, to which she only replied with a winking emoji.

He hadn't wanted their dinner to end so soon, especially not the way they'd left it. Salvador was comfortable in his own skin and not interested in whatever reactions people might have to his sexuality. Most people, however, were people that he didn't have a past with. That made Yara a special case, and he found himself wanting to know her thoughts. Her reaction to his coming out to her had been instant, the surprise on her face interrupted by the emergency that had brought here. What had she been about to say?

Being queer had lost him friends, growing up in a time far less tolerant than the one he experienced now. But there was no way Yara would be one of them, right?

There was still a significant amount of discomfort between them, the abrupt ending of their relationship hanging between them like a shadow. Salvador was constantly reminding himself to keep on his guard. The moments where he forgot about that, where he let the ease and familiarity of her presence envelope him with gentle warmth, were dangerous. He could not let himself feel any of that.

Salvador watched as Yara stepped closer to the patient's bed. Mr Orlay was much paler than he'd looked when he had finished the nerve conduction velocity test, a sheen of sweat covering his face, his chest slow to rise.

'Good evening, Mr Orlay,' she said as she approached his bedside. 'The nurse watching you paged me about your complaints. I know it's a bit of a pain, but could you walk me through it as well? I'd like to hear it first-hand.'

She smiled reassuringly as Mr Orlay went over his symptoms, showing her where he'd lost feeling in his fingers and arms. Yara went along as he described everything, her gentle touch confirming the pain points. Occasionally she'd stop, as if to commit some important detail to memory before she went back to the patient.

Watching her work unearthed a whole different dedication and talent in the medical world. Everyone Salvador had ever worked with at this hospital had been a prime example of patient care and responsibility.

It only enhanced and highlighted the worrisome connection snapping into place between them—now that the obstacle of her supposed marriage was out of the way. His brain had latched on to this information, playing it over and over in his head when it didn't even matter. Just because she was available didn't mean *he* was.

Salvador perked up when Yara disengaged from the patient, stepping back to him. 'You were watching,' she said, with a hint of amusement in her voice.

'I was.' His voice sounded a lot huskier than he intended it to be. Watching her work had been fascinating, every action taken with such deliberation and care for her patient.

'So, what do you think?'

'That you are a brilliant doctor.' The words

manifested in his brain and a moment later tumbled out of his mouth with no further prompt.

Yara turned her head around to look at him,
her brown eyes wide, and, despite the dim light
of the patient room, he noticed a faint blush
kiss her cheeks—bringing the desire he had
pushed down back to the surface. His hand
twitched, yearning to reach out and brush his
fingers over her face. Would she be as soft as
she looked?

'I meant with Mr Orlay,' she said as she
pushed him out through the door so they could
have their conversation out of earshot. 'What
do you make of his symptoms?'

'Oh…' Of course. What else would she be
talking about? They were here to see to their
patient. He leaned against the wall outside of
the room, crossing his arms in front of his chest
and looking upwards, thinking. 'Weakness in
his extremities should have dissipated at this
point, but it might still relate to his surgery.
Cardiac tamponade?'

Yara tapped her index finger against her
cheek while following his gaze and searching
the ceiling for the answer to the medical mystery presenting itself.

'Cardiac tamponade can be gradual, though after surgery I would have expected it to be rapid,' she mused.

'We could ask the cardiologist to do an EKG on him. Though he won't be in until tomorrow. I can page the on-call person in the department.'

Yara shook her head. 'I don't think it's a tamponade. Let's do a Doppler ultrasound instead and see what the blood flow to his extremities looks like.'

'Right now?' he asked, his eyes darting to the clock on the wall. The evening had already progressed way beyond what he'd expected, but what he found most concerning was how much he wanted her to say *Yes, right now.* So that their time together wouldn't end.

How strange things had turned out. Seeing her two days ago had shaken his world upside down, bringing back all the hurt and fury she'd put him through when she faded out of his life. But beneath that, he'd found all the other emotions he'd lost as well—including this deep connection they had once shared where they could say anything to each other. Salvador hadn't expected that to come rushing back when he felt the anger surge. But there it was. Tiny and so fragile, but it had survived inside his tormented self.

Yara followed his gaze to the clock and closed her eyes for a second. She hadn't realised how late it was. Mr Orlay was stable; his condition had worsened, but not to the extent that he needed immediate intervention.

'I didn't notice the time. You need to get back home to your nephew, and I have some research to do,' she said, and glimpsed the hint of an expression fluttering over Salvador's face. Was he disappointed their night was over? Or was that some needy part of her brain playing tricks on her?

'The babysitter is around for another couple of hours. We can go over your plan for the morning if you'd like.'

Her heart skipped a beat, tumbling inside her chest as if she had missed a step on the stairs. Did he want to stay with her longer? 'Okay, that sounds good. I have just the right snack.'

Yara waved him along until they reached her improvised office. She led him in, closing the door behind her, and marched over to her handbag. Smiling broadly, she took out a rectangular slab and put it on the table before taking the seat next to Salvador.

He looked at the table and then at her with a raised eyebrow. 'You carry bars of chocolate around with you?'

'*Swiss* chocolate,' she said as she reached for the wrapped bar, prying it open and breaking a small piece off to offer it to Salvador. 'I was there a couple of weeks ago for a case and just never took it out of my bag.'

'You are just as chaotic as I remember,' Salvador said as he nibbled on his piece of chocolate as if she had offered him some unknown substance he needed to analyse before putting it anywhere near his mouth.

'Glad to hear that the only thing that's changed about me is the number of wrinkles and grey hairs.' She made a joke to deflect the sudden awareness his words caused to stir in her veins, the few handspans of air between them suddenly not feeling like enough distance.

'I think they suit you,' he said in a low voice that vibrated through her every bone.

Was he...flirting with her? Impossible. The conversation they'd had at the diner came rushing back to her, the surprise at his revelation at the forefront of her mind. Salvador's last relationship had been with a man—changing her perception of their past relationship.

Had he already known back then? That would take some of the sting out of her past decision. If they'd never had a chance, her family's pressure was still appalling, but at least she could cope with the regret, knowing they were never meant to be.

If Salvador could have never loved her the way she had yearned for him to, maybe there was no risk in telling him the truth about her feelings for him—because there were no *what-ifs*. She could get this weight off her chest and absolve herself from her final regrets.

So had she been imagining the tension swirling around them ever since she came back as well?

'I have to tell you something,' Yara said, before she could change her mind.

He raised his eyes from the piece of chocolate pinched between his fingers, his expression expectant without the hint of anything else, just waiting for her to say what she wanted to say.

'I said I'd be honest with you, so…when I left

for med school, I *wanted* to be with you. I still panicked and treated you in an unacceptable way. But it wouldn't be right for me to pretend that I didn't want our relationship to change. I did…want it, that is.'

Yara didn't dare to look at him. Instead, she kept her eyes trained on the bar of chocolate on the table, her fingers woven into each other to stop her from fidgeting.

'Why did you say something else two days ago?'

Her eyes shot up, not expecting the question. Why did *that* matter? If he wasn't interested in women, why would he care about whatever she'd felt for him ages ago? Yara still was sure she could tell him about her parents' influence, how she had so willingly surrendered agency over her own decisions.

'That's a lot more complicated than I can explain…' Her throat bobbed when she swallowed the lump building in her throat.

'Try me.' He pushed his chin out in a non-verbal challenge.

'I…' Yara hesitated, unsure what to say next. Telling him one piece of her truth had been hard, but the lightness following her words freed up the pressure around her chest, easing her into a comfort with him she hadn't expected—and worse, it only strengthened the irresistible pull coming from him.

'I let myself believe that my parents had my best interests at heart, and it's only been in recent years that I realised they hadn't thought of me as much as of the perfect family picture they wanted to put on their mantelpiece.'

The words bubbled forth the moment she had decided to share this piece of her as well. The warmth radiating from his eyes set her at ease, creating a glowing spark in her chest that banished the tension. It was as much as she dared to say. Even though she resented her parents for all they had put her through, she couldn't expose them as such manipulative people to Salvador. What would he think if he knew how easily they had manipulated her?

Salvador remained silent, and when she looked up to meet his gaze her breath caught in her throat at the intensity of the gleam in his dark eyes. There wasn't a trace of a smile at the corner of his mouth. No tell-tale twitch to indicate how amusing he found her past choices. His features seemed hewn from stone.

'You wanted to be with me?' he finally said, and the rasp in his voice sent signals firing to all of her nerve ends. Signals she *shouldn't* be firing because he wasn't available to her.

'Yes,' she said with a shaky voice, waving her hand to deflect any deeper digging into this. 'Now I understand I could have saved both of us a lot of pain by just being honest. I mean, I know now that you would never have been interested in me—'

'Why wouldn't I have been?' The question threw her off guard. It didn't seem to fit into the flow of conversation. Was he going to pretend as if he hadn't come out to her?

'Because you...date men.'

Salvador exhaled through his nose in an audible sigh, crossing his arms as he leaned back. His eyes didn't leave hers as he rolled his jaw, seemingly contemplating his next words.

A thought popped into her head that made her bite her lower lip. Had he not meant to out himself to her? Had this been a slip of the tongue and she was putting him on the spot? 'If I've made—'

'I'm bisexual.'

And just like that the record playing in her

head scratched again, leaving her in complete silence as his words sank in.

Bisexual.

He dated men…and women.

'Oh, no…' she whispered, more to herself than to him, as the awareness of his proximity flared up again, cascading through her body and setting fire to the deepest layer of her skin.

'I struggled with it for a bit, but I can assure you it's true.' This time there was a smirk building in the corners of his mouth and amusement shone through his voice.

'No, I meant that I…' She didn't know what she meant. This wasn't going according to plan at all. They were supposed to joke about her falling for him and move on. Now everything inside her was roaring back alive, and she didn't know what was true and what wasn't. The picture in her head of Salvador changed, bending under a new reality that had been thirty years in the making.

'Does that change how you see me now?' he asked, as if reading her thoughts.

She paused, giving her brain a moment to catch up to the changing information and how it put everything she knew about him in a new perspective. After a few breaths, she shook her head.

'It doesn't change how I felt about you.'

He had never even hinted at questioning his sexuality when they were together.

'I didn't know until a few years later, though I can't say if it had impacted our relationship or not. Since you were gone, I didn't have to explore my sexuality in the confinement of a monogamous relationship.' His words were gentle, and yet Salvador didn't show a hint of his emotions on his face as he spoke.

'It doesn't bother me, if you're asking that. I'm glad you felt comfortable enough sharing that piece of you with me,' she said after a moment of quiet. 'Maybe I would have done something similar if I hadn't got married so young…'

Her voice trailed off. Thinking about the people Salvador had been with instead of her chipped at a hidden part inside her chest, hurting more than was appropriate in this situation. After all, she had been the one to leave and give him that freedom.

'Do you still like me the way you did when you left?' His voice was a low grumble cutting through her defences and landing right in the spot behind her navel, where the force of all her feelings was accumulating.

'Salvador...' His name dropped from her lips in a nervous chuckle that vibrated through the tense air between them. He looked at her, his eyes alive with an unknown fire that sent a tremble tumbling down her spine. 'I don't know if...'

'Because it's only been two days since you came back into my life and you've slipped right under my skin, Yara,' he said, and the gravel filling his voice pulled hard on the pinch in her stomach she was trying to fight off. 'Whenever I think about you my veins blaze with anger and hurt, yet I cannot stop thinking about you to save my own life.'

'What?' Something inside Yara cracked at his words.

A thousand different scenes popped into her head, all of them depicting what life with Salvador by her side could have been like, and her heart split under the pressure of that vision, of what they had lost without even knowing. Were those visions even realistic, now that she knew about his sexuality? Or had it been necessary for her to leave so Salvador could become the man he was now?

It didn't matter at the moment, when he was getting so close that she felt his breath sweep over her hot skin.

Salvador's hand went up to her face, tracing an invisible line from the highest point of her cheek down to her chin. His thumb moved up, brushing against her lips and leaving a searing hot sensation where he'd just touched her. Her body responded instinctively, yearning to fulfil a dream she'd kept alive inside her memory for many years.

'You destroyed me when you left, and I haven't forgiven you for what happened. Despite that, all I want to do in this moment is kiss you,' he said as he brushed his finger over her lips again. 'How are you doing this to me?'

'Salvador…' This time his name was not a chuckle but a plea, and a moment later he closed the gap between them and brushed his lips against her in a kiss she had been imagining for almost all her life.

When they had started their conversation, Salvador had not expected to kiss Yara by the end of it. Her confession had thrown him for a loop, and he still wasn't sure that he had processed everything she had said. His affection for her had been a low-humming being living inside him, sent into a deep sleep over the years—but always there. He just hadn't been able to sense it over the hurt her leaving inflicted on him. But as he touched her lips, it roared alive with a frightening intensity.

He wanted to rip the clothes off her body and have his way with her right this second. They'd lost years to meddling and insecurities, stopping them from ever realising their true potential.

Though he knew that he had ultimately needed to be on his own to explore who he really was, he still lamented the future they had never had. But she had left him broken, his trust in people's intentions never truly recovering. The walls he had built because of her abandonment were created out of steel. Nothing could tear them down, not even the woman he'd wanted so fiercely.

The scars in the depths of his soul had never quite healed. Yara had cut him out of her life without a second thought. She had told him why and the closure helped to put things into context. But the truth had not undone the damage—and a part of him wondered if it could ever *be* undone.

But despite the fury still fresh in his mind, the desire for Yara exploded through his body. They may not have a future, but maybe he could permit himself to trust her enough to fulfil a fantasy he'd carried around for years. One he could sense bubbling beneath her skin as well as she leaned into his touch, grasping at him with an urgency reflected in himself.

The way she moaned against his lips as he deepened their kiss almost made him think there was a path to repair his trust in her. The feel of her body against his blanked out all the pain and anger, and he gave in to the pull, even if it was just for a moment. Tomorrow they could go back to professional courtesy—in this moment he wanted to draw back the curtain just a little and glimpse the life they had never had.

Yara's hand came to rest on his chest as he pulled her closer into his arms, the other one grazing over his thigh, which sent a jolt of excitement through his system. He was an adult man with plenty of experience, yet a kiss and the prospect of what he would find beneath the layers of her clothes alone left him hard and aching. He wanted to have her, even if it was just for this night...

The thought lingered on the edge of his mind as his mouth left hers, feathering indulgent kisses over her jawline and down her neck.

'Salvador...' Her voice sounded airy, as if she was somewhere far away.

He smiled against her skin when he felt a shiver rock her body along with a high-pitched hiss as he nuzzled underneath the neckline of her blouse, relishing the softness of her skin.

'Salvador, your...' hearing his name from her lips in the state they were in sent another jolt coursing through his veins, bringing the need for her to an excruciating level '...your phone.'

She pressed the words out between shaky huffs that almost drove him to the very edge of existence. 'What?' His mind was murky, wrapped in a luscious cloud of her scent and the burning in her eyes that begged him not to stop.

'Your phone is vibrating,' she said and managed to bring him back to reality. His phone? Who would try to reach him at this hour?

Felix. The thought startled him back into reality, as if someone had doused him with a bucket of ice water. The air of attraction around them vanished and rational thinking kicked back in as he brought some distance between them.

Yara's eyes were wide, the fire he'd seen in them mere seconds ago extinguished.

He reached for his phone on the table and noticed the time. Just past midnight. He'd told Ciara he'd be back home an hour ago. 'I have to go. The babysitter needs to leave,' he said with a sigh and looked at Yara.

She'd retreated from him—both physically and emotionally, as he couldn't glimpse the moment they'd shared in her expression. Where the fire had burned thick walls stood now, impenetrable and devoid of any hint he could latch on to.

Regret uncoiled itself in his chest. *You stupid, stupid man.* He'd lost control for one second, and it had been enough to throw the rest of their professional relationship into the fire. Only for the fulfilment of a fantasy he knew could never become reality.

Not with his life the way it was. Not with who he was.

'You okay getting back to the hotel?'

Yara nodded, her face remaining expression-less.

He didn't want to leave. His feet remained rooted to the spot, even though he gave them the command to move. Salvador wanted to stay, to be with this woman who had slipped back under his skin as though she had never left, driving him up the wall with unresolved desire.

But *wanting* wasn't enough—and he wasn't even sure how much he truly wanted this and how much were ancient feelings stirring in his chest.

'I'll see you tomorrow for the ultrasound, yes?' His words were meant to gauge her re-action, give him some clue about what had just happened with them.

'Tomorrow, yes. Goodnight, Salvador.' She avoided his gaze as she spoke, her face blank and unreadable. Not a good sign.

Hearing his name from her lips this time didn't set his blood alight, but instead pawed at the wound he'd hidden away since they'd last spoken to each other.

What an unnecessary and difficult situation he had just plunged himself into because of his poor impulse control, he thought as he left the office to hurry back to the one person who needed all his effort and attention right now— Felix. The one reason he should have stayed away from Yara and the ancient beast she had awoken inside him.

CHAPTER SIX

WITH A DEEP BREATH, Yara calmed her roiling nerves and pressed the doorbell. For the next couple of seconds there was silence behind the door, then she heard shuffling, followed by the clicking of a key being turned in a lock.

The door swung open, and Yara stared into the surprised face of her sister, Bianca.

'Yara, what the—?'

'I kissed Salvador last night.'

Bianca's mouth fell open, and she blinked at her several times as she struggled with comprehension.

'Right...' The word came out elongated as her thoughts caught up with her. 'Lots to unpack here.'

She stepped to the side, inviting Yara in.

Even though it had been a few years since she'd last been to Brasília, Yara found comfort in the fact that Bianca's house still looked the same. Life around her may be ever-changing, but she knew her spot on her sister's couch would be waiting for the exact moment that she needed it. Like right this moment, when she had just kissed her high-school sweetheart.

She heard Bianca potter around in the kitchen for a couple of minutes, and when she appeared through the door she was holding two steaming mugs. She handed one of them to Yara and held on to the other one, taking her seat on the couch.

'So... You and Salvador are a thing again?' Bianca asked, and Yara almost choked on her tea.

'No! Do you think I would storm into your house on a random morning if I got back together with him?' She paused, the aroma of chamomile wafting up her nose and calming some of her jumbled thoughts. 'And I don't think you can call it *back together* when we hardly dated. Mum saw to that.'

'We are Lopes women. We can't be seen consorting with vagabonds,' Bianca said with a knowing nod.

Yara sighed into her tea. 'Are you planning on being at all helpful? I need to know so I can adjust my expectations.'

'Sorry, sis. I had to tease you a bit for not telling me that you're back in Brasília.' She gave her a chiding look. 'But all right, let's have it. Why are we kissing old flames we haven't spoken to in three decades?'

'I don't know…' Yara looked down at her tea, her chest expanding with a long breath that left her body in a drawn-out sigh. 'We were talking about our time together, and I wanted to tell him the truth about what happened between us when I left for med school. It turned very nostalgic, and then he told me…'

Yara interrupted herself, masking the unnatural pause by taking a sip of her tea. She had almost blurted out the news about his sexuality as though she were some common gossip. While his sexual identity was closely linked to their relationship, she didn't feel as if she had the right to out him to anyone who wasn't of his choosing.

Bianca furrowed her brow, thankfully not noticing her abrupt stop. 'You are too far ahead of me for me to understand the story. Why are you here? And how did you end up kissing *another man*?'

She looked at her sister, the raised mug stopping halfway to her lips. In the chaos of her own inner turmoil about Salvador, his confession and their kiss, she hadn't even realised that Bianca didn't know *any* of the steps leading up to the terrible decision of kissing him. Yara was so used to her sister knowing things about her, she hadn't really noticed how that closeness had changed over the years.

Yara had spent several years travelling for work and establishing her career the way it was now to escape her marital home. She could have come home, but some remnant of the pressure her parents had put on her stopped her from confessing what had happened. Instead, she pretended that everything was fine when she spoke to her sister, and avoided Brazil even though it hurt her to stay away.

She took a deep breath. 'Lawrence and I got divorced.'

Quiet tension slipped into the space around them as Yara awaited her sister's reaction, unable to tell what it would be. She wished Bianca would have had an instant reaction—big and angry. That was something she knew how to deal with. Quiet was so much worse than anger.

'When?' was all her sister asked, her expression suddenly so serious that a shiver trickled through Yara's body.

'It was finalised last year, but we separated a few years before that.'

'When you started travelling more...' Bianca mumbled, and from her expression she could tell that her sister was putting the timeline together. 'But you struggled before you got to that point.'

It wasn't a question, but Yara nodded anyway. That was when she'd isolated herself from her sister more and more.

'Yes. I was never in love with Lawrence. Not really. I thought I was, but it turned out that even if you want something to be true, it doesn't make it so.' For years, Yara had operated on autopilot, going through the motions as she and Lawrence led separate lives. She had thought she'd lost the ability to feel anything any more, getting too lost in a marriage that wasn't meant to be.

Until a few days ago, when she'd first had a moment alone with Salvador—and since then the air in her lungs had tasted different, fresher.

That observation had driven her into seeking out her sister today. Her feelings for Salvador morphed into more than just ancient memories and attraction, but something tangible and real—if she was brave enough to reach out and grab it.

And she needed someone to talk her out of it.

'Is that why you're kissing Salvador all of a sudden?' Bianca asked, and Yara almost laughed because even though she'd asked herself that same question, the impact was different when hearing it in her sister's voice.

'No… Kissing him wasn't part of any plan.'

'I'm still not sure why he's a part of this story.'

'Oh, right…' Another detail she'd skipped over in her desperate need to get straight to the point. 'He works at the hospital that hired me.'

Bianca put her empty mug down on the coffee table, and it was only then that Yara realised how much time had passed. The steam had stopped rising from her own tea, the ceramic mug now cool against her skin.

She wasn't any closer to finding a solution to her problem.

'How long are you staying here?' her sister asked.

'Only as long as the case lasts. Probably no longer than till the end of next week.'

Bianca nodded. 'So you don't really have enough time to get yourself into too much trouble with Salvador.' She paused with a smirk. 'Mum will not be happy about this.'

'Mum will feel nothing about this because we're not telling her,' Yara said through gritted teeth, glaring at her sister.

'Please invite me to the conversation with her when you tell her that you and Salvador ended up back together.'

'I *cannot* be with Salvador, no matter what I *want*. This was just a kiss!' Her heart slammed against her ribs, her pulse thundering through her body. The denial crossed her lips before she had the chance to process it.

The words rang in the silence between them, their heaviness settling in the pit of her stomach in the form of an icy boulder. That was the truth Yara had struggled to come to terms with over the last days. She couldn't believe how fast her desire for Salvador had re-emerged, rearing its head the second she let her guard down just a fraction. After thirty years, the spell he had put on her hadn't disappeared, but rather lain dormant in her, just waiting for a chance to erupt. Meeting him again had been too easy, their connection clicking back into place when they worked through the discomfort and awkwardness.

Maybe she had done well in leaving, giving him the space he needed to become who he was. She didn't know what their relationship would have looked like if she hadn't left. Would he have resented her for keeping him from exploring what was within him?

The idea that her mistake might have helped him learn about the facts of his sexuality was strangely calming.

'Why not?' Bianca finally said into the quiet, asking the question Yara didn't want to answer.

Yara gritted her teeth. 'I just can't. My life is not here, and he has his nephew to take care of. We can't go back and pretend nothing happened.'

'Is that really how you feel, or are those just the reasons you were able to come up with in the heat of the moment?' Her sister scrutinised her, and Yara shivered under her knowing gaze, probing into places she didn't want any light shed.

The coffee table groaned when she slammed her half-empty cup onto it with a bit too much force. This wasn't the conversation she was ready to have right now—or ever. 'I can't deal with this right now. I came here for some help, not to be talked into something I can't have.'

Bianca sat back, watching her with intent. 'I'm not trying to talk you into anything. Just trying to give you some perspective, okay? Now, sit back down.'

Yara glanced at the screen of her phone. 'I have to go and check back on the patient. We've started him on some new medication.'

Her sister recognised her words as the excuse that they were, but she nodded anyway, getting to her feet herself. 'You're off the hook for the lecture this time, but you'd better come for another visit before you leave for your next assignment, you hear that?'

An involuntary smile curled Yara's lips, and she nodded. 'I will.'

Salvador stepped through the doors of the emergency department at his hospital, and chaos erupted all around him. Nurses and doctors were shouting across different treatment bays, while monitors beeped with unrelenting intensity between heart wrenching-moans of the injured being delivered by the paramedics.

He immediately kicked into action, the reason for his visit forgotten as he realised his colleagues needed his help. He approached the trauma bay closest to him as they wheeled in an unconscious person lying still on a gurney.

'What happened? I'm here to help.' The junior doctor pushing the gurney glanced at the badge that hung from the breast pocket of his lab coat, then looked up at Salvador as if trying to confirm that he could be trusted. He couldn't blame him. As one of the high-ranking radiologists, Salvador hardly ever spent any time in the emergency department, only ever coming down here to fulfil some urgent requests of the chief.

'Bad accident on the highway near us,' the doctor explained as he started working on the patient. 'More ambulances on their way.'

'Got it.' Salvador turned around and headed to the entrance, stepping in to help the emergency department and its already thinly stretched resources.

On his way to the loading bay, he grabbed latex gloves, pulling them over his hands as the next ambulance arrived. The doors swung open as the paramedic jumped down, pulling the gurney out. Everything around him slowed when Yara's face came into focus. The paramedics' voices faded into nothing, replaced by the roaring static in his ears.

He froze as his eyes traced the splatters of blood covering her front, horror spreading through his body with each heartbeat. It wasn't until her brown eyes locked into his that he snapped out of his trance and realised that she was hunched over the patient with her hands over the wound.

'John Doe seems to be in his early forties, involved in a car crash at high speed,' the paramedic said as he pushed the gurney towards Salvador. 'Pulse is thready, and there is a large wound on the abdomen, already packed with antibiotics en route.'

'I'll take it.' Salvador nodded at the junior doctor beside him to help him as he grabbed the gurney, looking at Yara. 'Are you okay?'

She nodded, her eyes fixed on her hands where the white gauze she held against the patient's abdomen was turning bright red. 'I was a couple of cars down in a taxi when it happened, so I jumped out to help.'

The relief relaxing Salvador's muscles was pure and beyond any words. He didn't know how he would have reacted if it had been her on that gurney. The sense of undiluted dread that had gripped him when he saw the blood on her had rendered him immobile.

I've just got her back. Those were the words that echoed through his mind as he processed the scene in front of her.

They'd shared one kiss only, yet somehow it had affected Salvador to an unexpected level— just as seeing her in an ambulance had shaken him in a place he hadn't expected.

'Let's bring him into a trauma bay so we can get Dr Silvia off our patient,' he said to the junior doctor pulling the gurney ahead of him, who nodded and rushed out of the room to get the supplies needed.

'Place your hands over hers and press down,' Salvador instructed. 'Now, slowly draw your hands out from underneath, Yara.'

She did as she was told, slipping her hands out from under the grip of the other doctor, who continued to apply pressure in her stead.

Salvador reached his arm out to help her brace herself as she climbed down from the gurney and landed with a grunt on the floor.

'Okay, let's see what we have here.' He glanced at the monitors the nurse had just set up, checking the patient's vital signs with a frown. Yara appeared next to him a moment later, a gown pulled over her clothes.

'The fire department pulled him out of the passenger side of the vehicle,' she said as she circled around to the patient's head, checking the injury. 'Pupillary response is normal. No preliminary signs of brain trauma, but we should still order a scan.'

Salvador nodded and stepped forward to inspect the abdominal wound the junior doctor was still stemming. He moved his hand to the gauze and lifted it slightly. At some places, the deep wound had started to coagulate and stop bleeding, but it was too large and dirty to be cleaned and stitched here.

'Trauma Surgery will need to take care of this wound. Let's dress it up for transport.' He looked at the nurse typing on the patient's chart. 'Can you head out and see what the charge nurse wants us to do about this?' With this many patients coming in from the accident, there was bound to be a triage system set up already to prioritise which patient went into surgery first.

Salvador turned to Yara, who had finished placing a bandage around the patient's head. 'I can prep the wound for transport,' she said, and grabbed the supplies from the trolley when Salvador nodded.

He stood back as she took charge, lending a hand whenever necessary. When she'd diagnosed Dr Douglas's patient with a mere glance at the scans, he'd already known that he was in the presence of medical excellence.

What he witnessed now was her patient-care skills, working the bigger chunks of debris out of the wound and laying down gauze and bandages as they went around, saving the surgical team precious time they might need to check the patient for any internal injuries.

'Should we get an X-ray?' Yara asked, as if she was reading his mind.

He scrutinised the vital signs. The pressure on the wounds was keeping the patient from bleeding out, but the pulse was dropping. 'No, the surgical team will have to check for any internal damage with exploratory surgery. I don't think the patient is stable enough for any scans.'

Yara nodded and finished up the last bandages, before handing the patient over to the surgical trauma team, who transported the unconscious patient to the OR floor.

'On to the next one?' Salvador asked when the doors shut, and Yara nodded, a look of grim determination on her face.

CHAPTER SEVEN

AFTER TWO HOURS of lending a hand wherever needed, the workload in the emergency department returned to manageable, giving Salvador and Yara the opportunity to step away and clean themselves up.

In the rush of things, they hadn't been able to have a discussion or even acknowledge their existence to one another. The emergency had taken precedent, but now that things were quiet, Salvador became aware of the tension coiling itself around his chest once more—part longing, part fear of what the resurrection of his attraction for Yara meant.

The blood she'd been covered in while rendering first aid had dried under the gown and protective gear Yara had put on to help with the emergency. Salvador had led her to a private room Chief Sakamoto let his more senior doctors use to rest and refresh so she could get rid of the grime they'd accumulated on their shift.

Whoever had inhabited the office before it fell vacant must have spent enough time in that room, since they'd gone out of their way to make it cosy. The walls were painted in a darker grey tone that soothed any tiredness or irritation, and the couch on the far end of the corner had brought him through more than one late shift.

Though neither soothing nor comfort helped today as he stared at the closed door of the bathroom that seemed to mock the desire uncoiling in his chest. The thought of the state of undress Yara was in manifested in his head, driving heated blood to his groin, leaving him hard and aching. Even the dirt of an emergency-department shift did precious little to dampen the flame of longing stirring his blood.

Was she telling him to follow her? Or was that just a strand of misguided need for this woman weaving itself through his mind and making him see things that weren't there?

It must be the latter. Anything else was just not possible. Chance had brought them back together, even though Salvador knew they had no future. Not when his entire life was currently wrapped up in his nephew and choosing what was right for Felix over what he himself might want. He was not meant for the world she lived in, and hearing how easily her parents had convinced her of the same thing proved his point.

But dear God, he *wanted* her. The memory of their kiss still lingered on his lips, haunting him every time he closed his eyes to drift off. It was as if she had never left—never broken his heart. How could the short span of a week have fused them together again in such a profound way that Salvador hardened at the mere thought of her naked? Even the dread at the thought of her leaving didn't dampen his desire.

Or could he dare to taste what he couldn't have all those years ago? Wasn't that what was really happening between them? An ancient attraction they'd left unfinished, and now it was back between them, taunting him every time he saw her—coming between their work.

Salvador stood up, the couch moving against the wall behind him when he surged up. Two large strides brought him to the door leading to the bathroom. The water had stopped running, intensifying the image of Yara he'd conjured in his head, all wrapped in a luscious steam as she towelled herself dry, her hands slipping over the planes of her body he yearned to touch with such ferocity that his length flexed against the band of his trousers.

His hand hovered over the door handle, an internal debate raging on for what had to be eternity, sensibility trying to best the roaring in his chest.

Then he heard footsteps shuffle on the other side of the door.

Something was strange about Salvador when Yara came out of the bathroom dressed in a pair of oversized scrubs he'd given her to change into. Her clothes had become collateral damage after she witnessed the car accident on her way to her hotel, jumping out of the taxi to help the first responders. When she had stopped the large abdominal wound with her hands, she understood this would end up in a trip to the hospital for her. There was no way to dress such a wound in the field.

What she hadn't expected was Salvador on the other side of the ambulance doors, pulling at the gurney she had sat on.

The look of horror on his face had burned itself into her memory, burying a searing dagger between her ribs that filled her with unexpected waves of heat.

He'd thought it was her blood.

But they'd had no time to talk to each other with all the chaos in the emergency department, so they'd both sprung into action, working side by side—an experience that had affected Yara more than she had thought it would. While they were already working with each other on Henrique Orlay's case, that was somewhat different, as his role with that patient was very specific. He was there to interpret scans and results, feeding into her theories. In the emergency department today, she'd seen him in a different light. She had watched and supported as he worked with the trauma team to help everyone affected by the car crash. He'd worked with them as if he had always been part of the trauma team, not missing a single beat and showing great confidence in his ability to diagnose and treat patients under pressure.

It was a side of Salvador she hadn't seen until this moment, filling her with admiration for his dedication as a doctor. When she had pursued the idea of becoming a physician, that image was what she had in mind—strong and confident, but also flexible and kind, helping wherever necessary, with no ego involved. Her years of travelling had put her in front of a lot of different doctors and teams, each of them different in how they handled things. Ego and self-importance were things she had learned to deal with early on. Teams usually didn't like other people pitching in to their work—and that rule applied even more so to outsiders.

But no one had questioned or been bothered by Salvador's presence in the emergency department as he rolled up his sleeves. They were grateful someone was there to help in a time of crisis. An emergency department environment Yara could get used to.

'Are you okay?' she asked when Salvador remained unmoving, staring at her with a veiled expression.

He stood no more than two steps away from the door she had just opened, his posture stiff and frozen in place. Their eyes met for a few heartbeats, the intensity written in his dark gaze making the breath hitch in her throat. She watched as he took a slow step forward, followed by a quick one, and a moment later she was crushed against his strong frame as he hugged her close to him. Her arms hovered in the air for an undecided second, then her body went limp, giving in to the embrace. Yara wrapped her arms around his middle, drawing herself closer as she rested her face on his chest and soaked up the warmth coming from him as his scent enveloped her with the intimacy of their embrace.

She felt his nose on the top of her head as he nestled into her hair, his warm breath grazing over her as he drew her so much closer than she thought was possible.

'You scared me,' he mumbled, and all her senses had honed in on her body's reaction to his proximity, so that it took her several moments to comprehend the words he said to her.

'I'm fine, I promise. Scarier things have happened before,' she replied, listening to the strong beats of his heart against her cheek. All the reservations and uncertainty around their relationship were gone, replaced by the unyielding and intoxicating warmth his embrace caused to ripple through her. Even so many years later, his arms around her had the same effect on her—maybe even more, as she felt his closeness inside her core.

'Not to me.' His lips brushed over her hair as he spoke, each word creating a tiny kiss that sent sparks flying down her spine, lighting a trail of fires she couldn't control. All her senses focused on where his lips connected with her body, cascading the need for more through her.

Yara lifted her head off his chest and tilted it back to look at him. A heartbeat went by, tacit understanding passing through each of them as Salvador nudged her nose with his and angled his mouth over hers, before dipping down and drawing her into a kiss. It was different from the one they had shared two days ago. This one was filled with urgency and need, no longer bound by the restraints both had put on each other as they tried to establish their professional relationship around their old feelings of affection. No, this time around they both knew what they wanted—each other.

A thought that earlier in the day had sent Yara into a tailspin, rocking her so hard that she had to seek out her sister to clear her head.

Nothing changed between them, and her mind was still the same. Yara couldn't be with anyone else right now. She was still too damaged from a loveless marriage and years of manipulation, her trust in her own abilities so broken that she didn't know how to tell the truth of her feelings from wishful thinking. Was the growing attachment for Salvador real? Or was her affection for him no more than an echo of the love she'd used to have for him, and it would fade away the moment she looked too closely?

Was that even something *he* wanted, or was he acting on old feelings bubbling back to the surface? He'd been so angry at her when they first spoke here at the hospital...

Though those doubts floated in her mind, they faded into the distance when Salvador's teeth closed around her lower lip. The gentle bite rushed a wave of heat through her, setting the butterflies in her stomach on fire. She moaned against his mouth, opening her lips to his pleading tongue.

How could she ever have believed that what she felt in her marriage was enough? Even in the early days of their courtship, their passion had never run this hot. Yara had never felt as though she might cease to exist if she didn't give everything she was to the man eliciting such exquisite pleasure from her with no more than a deep kiss.

How would that mouth feel like on other parts of her body?

That thought almost undid her, sending a tremble through her that Salvador must have felt as well, for he lifted his head to look at her with passion-glazed eyes and heaving chest. He'd lost himself in that moment as much as she had—a fact that brought the tightness in her core to a new level.

'Are you okay?' he asked, the question dispelling some of the luscious fog surrounding them.

Was she okay? Probably not. Making out with her high-school boyfriend, who she had reunited with by chance after thirty years while also coping with the new reality of being a divorcee, didn't really spell stability of mind. But for the first time in ages blood was pumping through her veins, her senses alive. She dared to give in to a need she had denied herself for far too long—even if Salvador was a risky target to give in to, he'd also been the first one to penetrate the thick walls she'd surrounded herself with. And not even with stealth, no. He'd walked through the front gate as if he was simply coming home.

His hands were still planted on her back,

pressing her flush against him as he looked down on her with narrowed eyes that were filled with the same fog of lust and desire she felt inside her. Neither of them was thinking clearly, and that should be something that concerned her. But no matter how much she tried to push back on it, everything in her wanted to give in and get lost in the promise of pleasure his lips evoked.

His hands came to rest on each side of her face as he towered over her like a jaguar, looking down at its next meal after being starved for days.

Salvador grunted, taking another step forward so his entire body was covering hers as he pressed against her. His mouth nuzzled a spot behind her ear, his teeth raking downward over her skin to her neck. A firework exploded in the pit of her stomach, both because of the sensations his lips caused on her body and the intimacy of the situation. Her hips moved against him of their own accord and her eyes went wide when she brushed the apex of her thighs against his hardened length, straining against his trousers.

'This is what you do to me,' he said, to underline the truth of what she had just felt.

'Salvador...' She wove her fingers through his hair as his hands roamed over her body, finding the hem of the oversized shirt she was wearing and slipping beneath it. His fingers trailed her side, each brush stoking the fire in her core.

'This is all I've been thinking about for the last week,' he whispered as his right hand slipped to her front, palming her bare breast.

Yara instinctively leaned into his touch, writhing against him as pleasure thundered through her at this simplest of touches. She hadn't bothered to put on her bra after getting changed, thinking she'd be in her hotel room right now. Somehow, that decision had now worked in her favour.

'Me too,' she replied.

This had only been one of the many things she'd thought when it came to Salvador, but the only things she could remember were the riot of sensations the gentle brush of his fingers caused in her, and her sister's question that echoed in her head every time Yara thought she needed to put a stop to this: *Why not?*

What if she would simply enjoy what was happening in this moment without worrying about the future? Was there even a future to worry about? Before long she'd be on her way again, travelling the world to wherever difficult cases brought her. A life impossible to live for Salvador, who had his nephew to think about.

Their ideas of life didn't fit together any more, and maybe they never had. Would he have been able to be with the people he needed to be with in order to blossom into his sexuality if she had been there, holding him back?

If they both knew this was as far as things could get between them, was there any harm in giving in just this one time—as long as they were clear about their intentions?

'If we're going to do this…' Yara started, and then interrupted herself with a drawn-out sigh that tapered off in a longing moan when Salvador rolled her hard nipple between his fingers.

His mouth came back to hers, drawing her into another indulgent kiss as his other hand slipped further down, cupping her butt cheek and drawing her even closer.

'What are the ground rules?' he asked when

he finally released her lips with a huff of barely leashed desire.

'This is just finishing what we started some decades ago—the purpose is not to see if we could have made it as a couple.' Salvador looked at her with narrowed eyes that made a delicious shiver rake through her body, and it took every sliver of self-restraint she possessed to think about the rules of their engagement.

He nodded. 'One time. To get it out of our system.'

As if to emphasise his point, he let his hand wander to her front, moving beyond her waistband and between her legs. His fingers traced her through her underwear, finding the fabric beginning to soak with anticipation and need from nothing more than a few heated kisses.

Salvador must have thought the same thing, for he grinned with a dangerous spark in his eyes that curled her toes inside her shoes. This man was impossible to resist, and she didn't know how she'd walked away from him the first time around—or if she would be able to do it a second time.

'Oh, God...' Her head lolled back when his fingers brushed over her bundles of nerves, shooting lightning through her. He moved so slowly, each touch happening after extensive deliberation, and she raised her hips to meet him, urging him on.

But Salvador took his time, clearly enjoying this most exquisite torture he was putting her through. 'You ran away,' he whispered in her ear as he stroked her. 'Now you have to submit to my pace.'

Her eyes flew open when he withdrew his hands from her loose scrub trousers, passing the fingers that had just been giving her pleasure over his lips with an indulgent smile that made her heart skip a beat.

'When I finally have you, Yara, it won't be in an empty office at the hospital where I can't make you scream with pleasure without worry.' With those words he retreated from her, her personal space suddenly feeling empty and aching, the ghost of his touch still lingering on her flesh.

'Meet me at my hotel later?' she asked when he turned to leave. She wanted this so bad, every single nerve ending in her body was screaming at her to throw her arms around him again, and she knew if she let him walk out without knowing, she'd lose heart and it would never happen then.

'Let me make a call, see if I can get a baby-sitter to stay with Felix over the weekend.'

'Over...the weekend?' Yara's heart fluttered in her chest, and she tried swallowing the dryness spreading through her mouth. She hadn't thought this would last more than a couple of hours.

'I know just the place to take you,' he said, the gravel in his voice kicking her pulse into overdrive.

'Isn't that a bit much for a no-strings-attached hook-up?' Yara didn't know why she was poking holes in the plan when she really wanted to spend more than just a weekend with Salvador. So much more that she couldn't have.

The grin on his face turned to mischief, his gaze darting all over her body before landing back on her face. 'To get this all out of our system with one time, we'll need a whole weekend,' he said, and the unbridled hunger in his eyes set off another round of fireworks in her belly as she watched him turn around and leave. 'I'll pick you up tomorrow after work.'

CHAPTER EIGHT

THEIR WEEKEND DESTINATION was no more than an hour away from Brasília. If it had been just about reliving some fond memories, Salvador could have done it within a day. But he knew they needed more time than that if they *truly* meant what they had said about getting this attraction brewing between them out of their system by just letting go of their reins.

Salvador didn't know if this was the right approach or if the unrelenting need to have her—even if it was just for one night—was clouding his judgement to the point where he wasn't thinking straight.

Because he knew Yara had been right when they had spoken about their ground rules. This was a one-time thing that couldn't have a *Part Two* or *To Be Continued*. They were bold enough to let their desire take the reins for the duration of one weekend. After that they were nothing more than colleagues, working on a case together, and once that happened, Yara would be out of his life again.

The thought of her leaving so soon after they had reunited caused a sharp pinch in the centre of his chest that he didn't dare to examine much further. Until this week when she had appeared in his hospital, he hadn't known that he wanted her back more than he was furious at her—that his love for her had not died, but rather slowed down to an imperceptible simmer that had lain dormant in him for three decades, only to roar back alive when he first touched her lips.

A complication that just couldn't happen, no matter how he felt about it. He'd unexpectedly become a father to his nephew, and it was his responsibility to guide him through his life now without treading the path the rest of his family was all too eager to walk on.

There was also the small voice inside his head that understood her reluctance from thirty years ago. He didn't fit into her world, no matter how much he distanced himself from his parents' actions, proving to the world that he was different. They might be a lot older now, but Salvador still felt those shadows looming over him. Someone from Yara's background would always gravitate towards people like Lawrence Silvia, award-winning bio-engineer at a tech company that wanted to change the face of modern medicine.

His stomach dropped when he recalled the things he'd read about Yara's husband when he'd looked him up last night. Some sense of morbid curiosity had driven him to type Yara's name into the search bar, wanting to know more about who she had been married to—who was the man worthy enough for her to change her name to his.

Now Salvador knew so much more about her ex-husband than he ever wanted to know, putting him on edge. Something he didn't want to be, not for a no-strings weekend away from home. There was nothing at stake here. She would be gone in a matter of days, ending something that hadn't even started.

Yara gasped next to him in the passenger seat when she realised where they were going.

'Are we going to Lagoa Bonita?' Her head whipped around to look at him with bright eyes that made him want to pull over and have her right this instant.

'I couldn't let you leave Brasília without pitching up at our favourite spot.' When Salvador had bought his first car, they had taken regular trips over to Planaltina, walking around the shallow lake Lagoa Bonita that was located next to the small town. During the warmer season, the area was a popular destination for tourists as the lake was surrounded by pristine sandy dunes. The town was littered with small businesses and family-owned restaurants that appealed to both the locals who lived here to escape the bustle of the big city and also the visitors looking for a cosier experience than Brasília had to offer. Though it was Brazil's capital, much of the beauty and fun existed outside of the city's boundaries.

This late into autumn Salvador hoped that things would be calmer around here, even though he hadn't really planned on letting her leave the bed once she was in it.

'I wonder how much it has changed over the years. Do you know if they still have that small beach bar on the shore of the lake?' Yara looked at him with a sweet smile that caused his heart to leap against his chest. He remembered the bar she mentioned. They'd spent weekends there, enjoying mocktails as their friendship blossomed into something more.

'I don't know. I haven't been back since my brother's sentencing...' His voice trailed off.

Yara looked away for a moment, watching the landscape pass them by in a mixture of green and brown colours.

'How is Henrique doing?' he asked, to change the topic and bring some levity back into the conversation. Work was always the safe option for them.

'He's been very cooperative around the diagnosis. Taking him off all medication has not been easy, but he gritted his teeth through it and we gathered some useful insights. Somehow his immune system is attacking his peripheral nervous system.' She turned her head back at him, her finger tapping against the side of her nose. 'I took a deep dive into his family history and didn't find anything hereditary that could link to his symptoms. So we are down to a handful of neurological diseases that can cause this.'

'He has an autoimmune disease?' Salvador

asked, and the gravity settling in between them gave him the answer. Autoimmune diseases didn't have a cure. Their only recourse here would be to teach Mr Orlay how to live with his symptoms as well as a life full of medication and regular check-ups.

'Unfortunately, yes,' she confirmed with a nod.

'It must be tough sometimes, being the bearer of so much bad news,' Salvador said after a few moments of silence as he processed the information about his patient's progressing diagnosis. 'You're brought in for the cases where the team has explored all the options and still comes up short. Which means you probably diagnose a lot of diseases that are hard or impossible to cure. They wouldn't call you in if they already knew the answer.'

'It can be hard, yes.' Yara sighed, and, acting on instinct, Salvador reached out to grab her hand with his free one, drawing it closer to him to comfort her. 'I count finding the right diagnosis as a good outcome, otherwise I would rarely feel good about my work. If I've found the right answer, that means the patient can get the treatment they need or at least some closure.'

She wiggled her fingers, weaving them through his, and squeezed his hand. It was a tiny gesture, but so loaded with affection that Salvador's chest tightened.

'Was all the travelling hard on your marriage?' That wasn't the question he wanted to ask.

No, what he really wanted to know was how any guy could be insane enough to let this woman slip through his fingers. But he couldn't say that to her. He was already too attached to her on an emotional level. He couldn't let her know about the depth of his affection towards her. What if she left again the way she had thirty years ago? Or worse, what if she felt the same way and didn't leave? There was no way of their being together without someone giving something up—and he could never ask something of this magnitude from her. Not when he knew he wasn't nearly enough for her.

'No, I think we stuck together for so long because we found a way where we didn't have to be around each other for much of the time.' It took her so long to reply that Salvador thought she had decided not to answer his question, deeming it too much of an intrusion.

Should he even be asking? His infatuation with her already bordered on something he couldn't commit to, yet when it came to knowing Yara again—learning what he'd missed in the years they'd not seen each other—he couldn't help but dig deeper and find out who she'd become, and discover fragments of her past he hadn't known about.

'I'm sorry to hear that,' he replied, throwing her a quick side glance. Their hands were still entangled, and he felt her thumb sweep over the back of his hand, drawing small circles.

'It's okay. I think it's time I talked about it to someone, and I'm actually kind of glad it's you.'

He raised an eyebrow. 'You haven't spoken to your family about this?'

'I mentioned it to Bianca when I went to see her the other day...' A noticeable hesitancy accompanied her words, as if she was choosing them with great deliberation.

'You decided to go and talk to her, after all?' He remembered their conversation on the first day and how she hadn't planned on seeing her sister while in Brasília.

Yara laughed, but it sounded strained. Her fingers kept dancing over the back of his hand. 'I kind of needed to explain why me kissing you wasn't a problem for my marriage—since I'm no longer married.'

Salvador didn't say anything to that, though a smile stole over his lips. That moment in the conference room seemed so long ago, even though it hadn't even been a full week.

He pulled into the driveway of a house off the main street and finally put his full attention on Yara. She was looking at the two-storey house with the light blue walls. 'This looks beautiful. How did you find this place?' she asked, her eyes still roaming the exterior of the house.

'It's mine. I used to stay here in Planaltina before I got custody of Felix. Since he's in the middle of a school year, I didn't want to take him away from everything he's ever known. Not with the amount of change he was already dealing with.'

He didn't often talk about Felix to anyone, not wanting to shine a light on the criminal record of his parents and brother. But Yara already knew about that and had never judged him for the actions of his parents, and he knew it wouldn't make her think less of Felix either. No, her eyes were full of warmth and understanding.

Had he made the wrong decision to bring her here? Somewhere that meant so much to him, to them? This weekend was supposed to be about sex and finally moving on from that phantom of a relationship that hung between them. They had this one step to complete, one they were both burning for. And then? Then Yara would leave Brasília and be out of his life again for ever. So the sympathy didn't matter, nor did the intense need gripping him whenever he was close to her. What he needed for Felix—and for himself, too—was stability, and she needed to be free to drift in and out of people's lives as she pleased. Or was there a way to combine both their needs?

Salvador pushed these thoughts away as he got out of the car. That wasn't a place he was allowed to go—ever. He would not let himself indulge in any idle fantasies just because the reality didn't live up to what he wanted it to be. This weekend with Yara, fulfilling the final step of what had been a slow-burn romance, would have to be enough. They wouldn't get a future together, so right now would have to suffice.

Yara's knees didn't quite hold all of her weight when she got out of the car and followed Salvador to the front door. They'd spoken so casually about their lives during the car ride, with her sharing things she didn't think she would—until those words had slipped right out of her mouth and into the open. The odd thing was that she felt relief to finally have admitted to an aspect of her marriage that had gone awry. That travelling the world had never meant to be such a big part of her career, but each time she had returned home she felt trapped in this farce of a marriage her parents had convinced her was what marriages were supposed to be like.

She'd come close to telling Bianca how she felt, believing her sister would understand, but her courage had thus far failed her. Even if her sister understood her, what if word got back to her mother that she'd not made the marriage she had been so keen on work? Though she knew

Bianca would never betray her trust, the news might slip out.

So many years later, she still felt the pressure of carrying her parents' ideal family picture on her shoulders, weighing her down. Until Salvador had come back into her life, and all she could feel now was this burning sensation of intense longing that could only be quenched by being with him. He had not judged her for her words, simply taking them at face value and believing her.

Her heart squeezed tight when she thought about his situation and how much judgement he himself had experienced throughout his entire life. Despite his family's perilous path, he'd given up his home to take care of his nephew while his brother served his sentence. A beautiful home, Yara noted as she stepped through the door, yet something crucial seemed absent.

The entrance of the house gave way to an open-plan living room, where a large, dark blue corner couch dominated the space. An empty vase stood on the glass coffee table and that along with the empty fruit bowl standing on the granite countertop of the kitchen island gave her an understanding of what was missing—a family to make everything come alive.

As it currently was it didn't lack any beauty, but it didn't feel *alive*.

'Did you live here with your ex?' she asked, looking for the traces of the man Salvador had been attached to in the past.

Salvador put his backpack on the floor as he locked the door behind him, looking around the place as if he hadn't seen it in a while. 'Ah, no. We lived in the city. I didn't know if Felipe would have to serve more time, but I knew my nephew would have to stay with me for some weeks until his father's sentencing. Edinho wasn't thrilled about that temporary arrangement, so when I got permanent custody of Felix we had to call things off between us.'

'He didn't want to accept Felix in your lives?' she asked, unable to comprehend this stance. If Edinho had really loved Salvador, wouldn't he at least try to make it work no matter what?

'Children hadn't been part of our plan,' Salvador said with a shrug. 'So it wasn't really a surprise for me that he didn't want to suddenly be in a relationship where a child was involved. The circumstances of our lives changed, and it was something he didn't want to commit to. It sucked, but I can understand his reasons.'

'That's such a mature way of looking at it.' Her heart cracked at the thought of him having to make such a decision on his own, as well as dealing with a pre-teen when he'd never had any children before.

'What about you?'

Yara's thoughts ground to a halt, and she looked at him in confusion. 'What about me?'

Salvador approached her with a faint smile on his face, coming close enough that she could pick up his scent of lavender and sea salt. He stopped only a few paces away from her, within touching distance.

'Did you want to have children?'

Her mind went blank for a moment, focused only on the air between them that became charged with energy, growing louder and hotter between them.

Children? That was a complicated and painful topic for Yara, and the last thing she wanted was the heaviness of her biggest regret weighing her down when they were supposed to be light—to have fun. This weekend wasn't about gaining some emotional closeness. The opposite, really—they had agreed to give in to the sexual tension that had been building between them from day one so they could finally get over it and move on.

'I...wanted to, yes. But it never happened. By the time I felt ready for children, my marriage had already deteriorated to the point where I couldn't possibly bring a child into such a situation. My parents were so clinical to each other, so focused on their perfect family picture that they didn't care about what that kind of cool detachment did to a child. I didn't want that for any child of mine.'

Salvador stepped closer when her voice faltered on her last words, laying the back of his hand against her cheek and gently stroking her cheekbone with his index finger.

'I didn't know that about your parents,' he said, his finger tracing a line down her jaw. 'Whenever I saw them at your house, they seemed like the perfect couple.'

Yara leaned into his touch, her eyes drifting close for one beat of her heart. 'They would never let anyone see the cracks in their marriage. I think that's the reason they were so adamant about who their eldest daughter picked as a spouse. The fear of what the neighbour would say if they saw me with—'

'With a ruffian like me?' Salvador finished her sentence.

With his finger under her chin now, he tilted her face upwards, grazing a soft kiss on the corner of her mouth.

Her heart slamming against her chest at the sudden closeness, she continued, 'I'm menopausal now, so I missed my window of having my own children, and I'm no longer sure if I even want to at this age.'

Ever since she'd left Lawrence, she'd thought a lot about adopting a child on her own. She'd wasted too much time waiting for the ideal timing that she lost her chance altogether. But she didn't want to be unfair to a child either. With the amount of travelling she needed to do for her work, it didn't seem fair to commit to a child when she was never settled in a single place.

Salvador stepped closer, eliminating the remaining space between them. His breath now grazed over her cheek as he angled his head down, brushing a soft kiss on her forehead. 'Strange. I never wanted children until Felix appeared in my life, and now I can't imagine what it would be like without him.'

'You don't have any regrets being forced to choose between him and your relationship?'

'There wasn't a choice. I could never abandon my nephew. After everything he's been through, he deserves some continuity and stability. I won't let anyone get in the way of that.' He said it with a finality that drove a sharp pain between her ribs, and she bit the inside of her cheek so as not to gasp.

Even though she knew it wasn't, it somehow felt as though this was targeted at her directly, as though she needed a reminder that their time together here was just about sex. It was what she wanted as well, right? It had been so long for her, the kisses they shared had been enough to open up a chasm of desire within her, just waiting to erupt from Salvador's touch.

Why were they even talking about children? That topic wasn't even near any foreplay-talk recommendations. Only this was another part of her she'd been too embarrassed to share with anyone, feeling so foolish about staying in the relationship that didn't fulfil her and give her what she wanted.

'He's lucky to have you,' Yara finally said, wrapping her hands around his midsection to pull him close against her. 'So, Dr Martins. I don't think you brought me here just to retrace my past decisions or go over yours.'

Somehow Salvador made it easy for her to share, to open up the gates on the imposing walls she had erected around herself—and that needed to stop. Sharing their innermost space wasn't necessary for that, even though it felt so right. But even though she had steeled her heart for this, words kept slipping out without a prompt, fusing her closer to the man she had slipped away from.

Salvador growled as his hands slipped around her waist to push her away from him and turn her around so her back was to him before he put his arm around her and pulled her flush against him. His lips brushed down her neck and to her shoulder, nuzzling into the silky fabric of the flowery dress she'd put on this morning for the car ride.

She shivered when his tongue darted over her skin, the fine hair along her arms standing on end as his intimate touch made the memories of her regrets sting less. This was where she was supposed to be—right in his arms, where nothing could touch her. Here she would only know affection and pleasure from the man she should have never rejected.

Her parents hadn't been concerned for her safety or wellbeing when they'd forbidden her to see him any more because of the criminal history of his parents. No, they had been worried about what people might say if their eldest daughter went out with the son of criminals.

But Salvador was nothing like them. He was kind and caring, pulling himself out from the toxic environment of his childhood home and managing to make something out of his life— even caring for his nephew in his time of need.

And now the hands of this wonderful man were gliding over her front, palming her breasts through her dress as his laboured breath swept over her ear. Something hard pressed against her, and she writhed at the anticipation of his length inside her. She moved her hips ever so slightly, grinding against Salvador behind her. The hiss escaping his throat turned into a groan that made Yara grin with delight. That she had that effect on him, even after all these years, caused such intense pleasure to ripple through her body that she felt her core contract, ready for what she'd been dreaming about.

The final step missing from what they'd had so many years ago. One night together—or rather one night spread over several hours of the weekend.

This was not at all going according to plan. Salvador had whisked her away to Planaltina to walk around Lagoa Bonita and remind both of them of the earlier days of their teenage friendship, before romantic roots had taken hold in either of their hearts. He had used to do this small trip whenever he needed to get away from his family and the damage they left in their wake. The lake north of the town was small and shallow, so the water was always warm enough to dip into if he wanted.

One day when he was sneaking away from class—his father had been taken to the police station the day before—Yara had caught him, demanding to know where he was going. When he had told her, she insisted on coming with him, not wanting him to go through any struggles alone. He'd always kept his family a secret, ashamed of their shady history and what that said about him, but even though Yara didn't know much about them, she lent him her support anyway.

Because that was exactly the kind of person she was—kind and thoughtful towards the people around her. He could see now that her upbringing had been as difficult as his, even if they grew up with a different background. Though she had made the choice to leave him, he knew the hints and machinations of her parents had driven her away from him.

Yara was a woman of remarkable calibre, and she deserved more than a passion-filled weekend—even though that was all he could give.

But the need to have her burned in his blood, circulating a dominating heat through his entire body with each beat of his heart, driving the fever pitch higher and higher.

Her butt pressing against his rigid manhood almost sent him into a red-hot frenzy, and he took a deep breath, letting his hands roam over her body, the silk of her dress cool against his heated skin.

'I was going to take you for a walk,' he whispered, despite having no intention of going for that walk any more. With one bat of her lashes, she had drawn him back under her spell.

'It'll be lovely after sundown, when the sand has some time to cool down,' she whispered, and Salvador hissed when she slipped her hand between their bodies, tracing the outline of his erection with two of her fingers.

'Skipping straight to the main event?' he asked through gritted teeth as she played with the button of his trousers.

'You know I've never been very patient. It was the one thing our teachers complained about.'

Yara pushed herself away from him and turned around in his arms, melting back into his embrace while facing him. The passion rumbling in his chest tore through his body when she locked eyes with him, a sensual smile on her lips that spoke of all the ways she wanted to have him.

Yara. The one who'd got away. The woman who had planted herself in his heart with such surety that even three decades later, the seed of it blossomed again after not even a week of being close to her. It was as if she'd never left, their connection as vibrant and alive as it had been all those years ago—his body still responding to hers with no more than instinct.

As if they had been made for each other.

'You are so sexy, Yara. Look what you do to me.' His hand slipped down her back, crushing her against him so that his full length pressed against her, twitching when he felt her shiver under his touch.

She tilted her head back in response, her fingers weaving through his dark hair and pulling his face down towards her mouth, meeting him with open lips for his tongue to explore. The last restraint on his desire snapped as their tongues tangled, taking their passionate kiss to new heights.

His hands came back to her front, finding the sash keeping her wrap dress together and pulling on it, need underpinning every move he made. When his fingers found bare flesh, he pulled away, unable to resist the temptation to finally look at her—a vision of Latin sensuality and beauty in the cream-coloured bra and panties combination she was wearing underneath.

A low growl loosened from his throat at the sight, his erection tightening even more. 'I've fantasised about seeing you like this for so long—and it doesn't even come close to what my horny teenage brain could come up with.'

Yara's eyes went wide for a moment, pink streaking over her cheeks at the unexpected compliment he'd given her, and he swallowed a disbelieving laugh. How could those words be something that made her blush? There was no way she hadn't heard these things before, was there? Or had her marriage really been just out of obligation and family duty?

It was in that blush on her cheeks as well as the tentative smile pulling at the corner of her lips that he realised how much damage her loveless marriage had caused her—how little she valued herself as a woman of tremendous beauty and sex appeal. Because Lawrence hadn't made her feel those things, she now believed Salvador's words to be no more than flattery.

One weekend might not be enough to change that perception, but he would try to give her this one thing before they had to go back to being strangers.

* * *

The look Salvador gave her made Yara feel light-headed. In all her years of marriage, Lawrence had not once looked at her like that.

She remembered her wedding night and the fear she'd felt at the lack of compatibility, seeking blame within herself—believing for a long time that she lacked something fundamental.

Now she knew that to be false, for Salvador's hands roaming over her naked skin set her entire being on fire—each nerve ending begging to skip ahead to the end, where she knew the culmination of many years of suppressed sexual desire lay, ready to burst apart at his touch.

Even with the temporary nature of their agreement, he took his time to make her feel at ease, giving her compliments she'd not heard in many years, and it hurt her to admit how much his hunger for her surprised her—to the point where she could hardly believe it, thinking it some farce that was a part of modern courtship.

Her dress fell to the floor with a hushed rustle, pooling into a heap behind her. The soft breeze coming from the open window caressed her skin with its warm touch, highlighting her state of undress. When was the last time she had stood in front of a man wearing nothing but her underwear?

He gathered her up in his arms with a reverent softness, his fingers moving over her skin, exploring every rise and dip of her body. When he unhooked her bra, he stepped back to let it fall on the floor. The look of excitement in his eyes made her laugh and roll her eyes at the same time.

'You've seen breasts before, Salvador,' she said, when he kept staring.

'But I've never seen *yours* before. They're like a work of art.' He stepped closer, his hands moving up her torso to palm her breasts, each thumb brushing over the peak of a dark brown nipple, sending an exquisite trickle down her spine and into her core.

She gasped at the gentle touch, her mind wiped clean of any second thoughts or doubts she had found there just a few seconds ago. All her senses were trained on Salvador and where their bodies connected. Her hands started to move on their own, finally freed of the restraints her overthinking had placed on them. They found the hem of his T-shirt, slipping beneath it to feel the warmth of his skin against her palm. His back was broad and strong under her fingers, and she pushed the fabric further up until he leaned back so she could pull the shirt over his head.

A smile like the one she'd seen on his lips just moments ago appeared on hers when she beheld Salvador's naked upper body. She had seen him like this before, but the memories of those occasions were nothing like the reality—probably because her desire for this man was at an all-new high. Salvador had been incredibly attractive as a young adult, and the years that had passed since she'd last seen him had only refined what handsomeness had already been there.

Yara bit her lip as her gaze wandered further down, her hand moving along his firm chest in unison with her eyes, drawing small circles in his chest hair before moving lower. She swept over this happy trail, following it to the point where it disappeared beneath his waistband.

'That won't do,' she mumbled, more to herself than to Salvador, flicking open the button of his trousers and pulling the zip down.

Salvador groaned when his trousers slipped down his legs, the only restraints on his erection now the fabric of his underpants. Yara brushed over the bulge with her hand and bit her lip when he flexed his hips in response, leaning into her touch with an enthusiasm that was foreign to her. Had anyone ever craved her touch this badly? Had she ever wanted to burn the way she was willing to in this moment?

The last remains of her hesitation fell away at the sound of deep and undiluted pleasure coming from Salvador when she touched him, daring to move the last barrier of clothing out of the way so she could wrap her hand around him.

'Deus... Yara.' Hearing her name from his lips turn into a moan set her blood ablaze, emboldening her in her actions.

She wrapped her hand around him, moving up and down in slow pumps, savouring each one as Salvador twitched under her touch. His breath left his nose in strained huffs, all his muscles tense as Yara placed her mouth on his collarbone, tracing kisses over the planes of his chest and down his abdomen to his navel.

When she sank to her knees, his strong hands wrapped around her shoulders as if bracing for what was to happen next. Her tongue darted over his tip, hesitant at first but then growing in boldness as Salvador's body moved under her touch, his throaty groans accompanying her moves as she drew all of him in.

His fingers dug into her flesh as she went on, her name clinging to his lips in a desperate plea for release that sent a shiver down her spine. Knowing the pleasure rippling through him was her doing, that she was the one shooting lighting through his body, easing and contracting his abdominal muscles with each sweep of her tongue over his tip—it almost undid her on the spot.

Yara let her eyes drift closed, relishing the feel of him against her, but the quiet moment lasted only a second before his hands tightened around her shoulders and a moment later she was pulled onto her feet, pulled out of the delicious stupor her ministrations had put her in.

The glazed look in his eyes as he crushed her against him brought another wave of heat to cascade through her body. His lips found hers, drawing her into a hurried kiss, tongues and teeth clashing, conveying the intensity of the fire she'd stoked in him with her mouth alone.

'I need to have you right now,' he growled in between kisses.

His hands found the seam of her panties, and one flick of his wrists dropped them to the floor. He pulled her into another long and indulgent kiss, his chest heaving against hers, then he grabbed her by the hips and lifted her up. Yara gasped when her feet lifted off the ground, and she wrapped her legs around him for stability as he carried her towards a large couch on the other side of the open-plan living space.

'On the couch?' she asked when she realised where he was carrying her.

'We'll spend enough time in the bedroom after this one,' he replied, a feral expression curling his lips upward.

Yara writhed against him as he walked her over, feeling his length press against her slickness, ready for him. But instead of pouncing on her when he dropped her on the spacious couch, he knelt on the carpet and grabbed her calves. She gasped in surprise when he threw her legs over his shoulders and seized her hips again to draw her closer to his mouth.

'What...?' The rest of her words died on her

lips, turning into a drawn-out moan when his tongue nestled into her folds, Salvador taking her like a man lost in the desert, finally finding an oasis to quench his thirst on.

'You thought I would let you have all the fun?' he said between licks, bringing her closer to the edge than she had been in years—and she was ready to go there with Salvador. Her muscles started to tense, the surrounding room drifting out of focus as stars began to dance in front of her eyes.

'Wait,' she huffed, pawing at his head until he appeared in front of her face. 'I want us to… together.'

Yara's senses came back to her as she examined her own awkward phrasing. Sex had not been part of her life in recent years, and when it had been it was with selfish lovers, who hadn't taken the time to give as much pleasure as they took. Already Salvador was so different from that, she didn't know how to react—had forgotten how to ask for a simple thing like that.

But Salvador, sweet and thoughtful, understood without her having to use many words. He scooped her into his arms, quickly lifting her again. As he held on to her he reached for the drawer of the side table, pulling it open and grabbing a condom that he pulled over his erection. He smiled when he was done and pulled Yara back on top of him. She had her legs on each side of his body, his impressive length strained against her, nudging in the right place and making her writhe with anticipation.

'Are you comfortable like this?' he asked as his hand came up to touch her cheek with a gentle brush.

Instead of replying, Yara angled her head down, drawing his lips onto hers and letting a passionate kiss do her talking. That he even bothered to ask showed her the man he'd always been and how big a mistake she had made when she let her parents convince her that there was someone more worthy out there.

He groaned against her lips when she released the tension in her legs, easing herself onto him. They looked at each other for a second as she settled down, an unspoken bond forging between them. All the words they'd been unable to say, all the dreams and plans of the future they had never got to have—these and more pictures floated in the tiny space between their bodies, hitching up her heartbeat until she could feel it in her throat.

So much lost that could never be recovered. But at least they would have this moment—this weekend—to live as if they had the rest of their lives together.

Pleasure mingled with the tiny needles of regret burying themselves inside her soul as they moved their hips together, their lips clashing and their breaths increasing, each thrust bringing them closer to the togetherness Yara had been craving the moment they'd started talking like friends again.

She gasped when Salvador picked up the speed, whispering her name into her ear as his hand slipped between them to stroke her as they both neared their climax together. Her hands dug into his shoulders, her head lolling backwards as her surroundings drifted away once more, making way for the moon and the stars twirling around in front of her blurred vision.

And when her climax arrived with an unexpected ferocity, interrupting the dance of stars with a powerful thunder blinding her to everything but the exquisite pleasure electrifying her body until she was nothing more than a bundle of frayed nerves—she screamed as Salvador had promised she would, both from the delicious torture raking through her body, and from how much her heart ached for him.

Yara realised, as he convulsed beneath her hands with the same kind of intense pleasure, that her insecurities around who she was had robbed her of the potential for something amazing—Salvador, who had found a way past her defences and was showing her a glimpse of what life could have been like.

What a cruel joke that she should get one weekend to pretend her affection for him could be more than just a fleeting moment. It couldn't, not with their lives being in such different stages. Not after she'd hurt him so much by abandoning him. A lifetime would not be enough to make it up to him.

But Yara decided she would give in, even if it was just for one weekend. Two days were better than none, and if she couldn't have the rest of their lives, she'd settle for forty-eight hours.

Anything to be with him.

If Salvador had thought that this would be enough to reset things between them, he realised late into the night how sorely mistaken he was. They'd made their way towards the bedroom eventually, getting drunk on their passion for each other until exhaustion had demanded its tribute and they'd passed out in each other's arms. As if they'd been meant to sleep like that all their lives and they just hadn't known.

Those thoughts darted around in his brain as he watched her sleep. He knew he'd gone too far when he pulled her tight against his chest, her perfect form fitting flush against his as if they were made for each other. With his chin resting on top of her head, he breathed in her scent, relishing the smell that brought youthful memories back into his mind.

Long-forgotten need stirred further in his chest—the exact opposite of what he had wanted to achieve with this weekend away. Finally sleeping with each other should have closed the circle, but instead it had just extended into a completely different shape, leaving him with a quaking heart and worry pulling at the corners of his lips.

No matter how fierce the yearning in his chest grew, they could only ever have this weekend. It was what they had agreed on, and he wouldn't let some wayward emotions lead him astray. Not when he was so alien to her world.

Though his feelings for her were changing—coalescing into something so real and tangible—he didn't dare to look at them for fear that his acknowledgment would be the missing piece that would break his resolve.

Their relationship had always been volatile, and Salvador needed calm and focus. Keeping Felix safe while dealing with the ongoing issues of his family was his number-one priority that he couldn't get distracted from. And Yara... She had her own life to live, outside of Brazil.

He would cherish this time they had together, but after that they'd have to go their separate ways again. If not... Salvador didn't know what he would do for her if he was brave enough to try—or foolish enough to let himself.

CHAPTER NINE

DESPITE HIS PLAN for a walk around the lake, they didn't make it out of the house that day. Both of them tried, each attempting to untangle their limbs from one another, only for the other to stop them with hunger in their eyes.

When Salvador had finally managed to tear himself away—from both the gloomy thoughts of the future and Yara's delectably soft and supple flesh—he made it as far as the en-suite shower before she found him, sinking back onto the floor and finishing the promise of pleasure he'd glimpsed in her when they first arrived at his place.

They ate their breakfast in comfortable silence, sitting close enough to each other that they could lean into the occasional caress. Nothing could disrupt their harmony—as long as they kept away from the fragility of their temporary arrangement.

'Still up to seeing Lagoa Bonita?' Salvador

asked when they had finished, pouring coffee into two travel mugs.

'Of course,' she said with a laugh so bright and full of joy that his knees grew weak for a moment. He wanted to hear that laugh for the rest of his life.

Only that laugh was not meant for him to keep, but rather borrow for the small amount of time they had left together, and he needed to remember that.

Despite the ongoing turmoil in his stomach, he reached out his arm and relished the feel of her dark skin against his when she draped her hand around his arm and let him lead her outside.

His house was close to the small lake, something he'd intentionally kept an eye on when he'd shopped around for a property. Though Lagoa Bonita was steeped in the memory of Yara and their relationship that had ended too soon, he'd still been able to enjoy the lake by himself on the rare days that he'd managed to go there—long before his nephew became his ward and he'd had some time on his own.

'Do you miss having time to yourself here?' Yara asked, as if reading his thoughts.

He looked around, taking in the neighbour-hood of colourful houses as they crossed the street until the grass turned to sand. 'Yes, I do—though I have no regrets about moving back to Brasília for the sake of my nephew. With Felipe being in and out of prison, along with the rest of his extended family, Felix needed stability more than I needed time to myself. Or a relationship, for that matter.'

The word *relationship* hung between them, highlighting the fragility of their arrangement and how much it pained him to think about it.

If Yara had noticed his hesitation around the word, she didn't let on as she said, 'I would have never thought that man trouble would be something we'd have in common.'

Her hand slipped down his arms until their palms lay against each other. She threaded her fingers through his, folding them over and gen-tly tugging at his hand as they continued their walk.

'I think I'm considered a bit of a late bloomer.' Like a lot of people in his community, Salva-dor had struggled at first, trying on a lot of different labels before he found the one that ex-pressed himself the best. Most of his youthful exploration had been so tied up with Yara and their developing relationship that he had never considered who or what else he might like until she was gone. Though her leaving was wrapped up in a lot of pain and regret, it had opened up a whole new world for him. One where he had found his tribe.

'How come?' she asked, genuine curiosity in her eyes. How was he supposed to explain that to her without sounding like a lovesick man who had sworn off women because of the one who'd got away?

That wasn't true, but Salvador would have to drag up a lot of exes to prove this point.

'I wasn't really interested in dating anyone after...' His voice trailed off. He'd started the sentence without thinking of how to finish it.

'After I left,' she finished for him, letting him off the hook with a small smile.

Despite their long conversation about moving on from what had happened, he still struggled to see completely past it when it had been such a painful time in his life.

'My father got into some more legal trouble when I was at med school, splitting my focus between studying and worrying about what madness Mum and Dad had got themselves into. So I didn't really get to think about my attraction to anyone until my first year as a trainee doctor in a hospital. And you know how much time we had to think about dating.'

Yara laughed, a sound like music drifting through the air. 'I was already married by then, but I slept in enough on-call rooms to know *everything*.'

'I saw male colleagues in secret first, unsure if I was straight, gay or just in the mood for something different. At that time my brother was the only person I had in my life with my parents in and out of prison, and he wasn't really the person to support his older brother through his sexual awakening.'

He paused, unsure if he had shared too much with her, if she even wanted to hear so much of his past that wouldn't have happened with her in the picture. But a curious spark lit up her eyes as she parted her lips and said, 'Did someone help you in the end?'

Salvador nodded, recalling his own struggles. 'I was always okay with the idea of being bisexual, but I became a lot more outspoken about it when Felix was born. I wanted him to have an uncle that was unashamed of who he was and whom he loved.'

'What about Felix's mother? You haven't really mentioned her.' Her tone was gentle, as if she wasn't sure if she wanted to ask the question.

Salvador shook his head. 'She's not around any more. Felipe says they knew someone was investigating them, so she took off. No one knows where she is, and she hasn't tried coming back for her son.'

'That's so sad for him...' she said with a frown.

He only nodded, and they remained quiet as they walked through the warm sand, the morning sun already bright in the light blue sky. They were in for a lovely day, Salvador thought, and that wasn't just because of the weather. He paused when Yara gasped. They had come over a sand dune and were now looking down at Lagoa Bonita. The water was of a deep blue in the middle and grew lighter the further out it went, the shallow edges of the lake mixing with the surrounding sand, shifting the hue of the water to a light green.

A few towels were spread around the sands,

with different sized groups of people clustering around each other, enjoying the final warm
days before the approaching winter would bring
a chilly wind to the lake. Salvador actually pre-
ferred the chill to the sunny days, simply because when there was no one around this place
felt like his own private oasis, where he could
withdraw and think.

Not that he got to do much of that since he'd
received custody of Felix.

He held on to Yara's hand as they sauntered
down the dune, placing the large picnic blanket
they'd taken with them near the shore so they
could look at the water while they sat. Salvador let out a deep sigh of contentment when she
sat down next to him, snuggling closer and laying her head on his shoulder as his arm came
around her side to draw her in closer. This—
sitting with her in this moment and enjoying
the morning sun over Lagoa Bonita—had no
business of feeling so right, so…meant to be,
when he knew this was no more than an illu-
sion, just waiting for the tiniest interruption to
cause the glass to shatter.

But even now he knew all of this, he couldn't
help but enjoy the moment as if it could last

for ever. For the first time in years, Salvador saw the world around him with clarity, as if he had needed her to lift whatever fog his family's trouble had enveloped him in. In one short week, she had become the missing piece, slotting into his life as if he'd just been waiting for her.

How was that even possible? Why now, when he was so wholly unavailable?

'What's on your mind?' Yara's question drew his attention away from his contemplations. His hand grazed up and down her arm, leaving tiny goose pimples in their wake.

'I...' He hesitated, looking for the right words to deflect that question. There was no way he could tell her about those thoughts. They had both agreed that this was nothing more than a weekend to 'get it out of their system'.

'How is Bianca doing?' He steered the conversation in this direction because that was what he wanted—to talk less about him and more about her.

The tension in her shoulders each time she mentioned her family was visible to anyone who knew how to read her, and apparently Salvador still very much knew how.

'She's Bianca, doing Bianca things... Though she's been looking after our mother ever since Dad passed away. After they sold the house, Mum moved into a gated community, and Bianca got a place near by so she could help her.' Yara stopped for a moment, smiling up at him. 'She's still working as a primary-school teacher, and also still trying to make it as an artist.'

This time Yara laughed, rocking into his body in a way that set his skin on fire again. After the rather sleepless night they'd had, he thought he might have been completely spent in the morning, but the river of desire for this woman was nowhere near stemmed, flowing through his body with each beat of his heart. If they weren't in such a public place, he might have climbed on top of her right at this moment.

'I'm glad she's always been happy with life in Brasília. It gave me the opportunity to leave and pursue what I was passionate about—to an extent, at least. My parents both had some rather strong ideas about what I should do with my medical degree.'

Salvador rested his hand on her stomach, drawing lazy circles with his fingertips. He remembered her parents having a firm grip on Yara and the decisions she made in life. When he'd met Mr and Mrs Lopes in their home so many years ago when he and Yara were just friends, he'd sensed their disapproving looks. They hadn't wanted their daughter to be associating with a 'street rat'.

It sounded as though her match with Lawrence Silvia had come from them, and that they had exerted quite a bit of influence over their daughter to get her to agree.

He was fairly new to the parenting game, but even so he could hardly imagine telling Felix who he should and shouldn't be with based on what *looked good* for the family name.

'So they wanted you to become a travelling diagnostician, or was that your idea?'

Yara stopped to think for a while. Not because his question deserved due deliberation, but rather because she had asked herself that question and come up short. She knew *she* had wanted to become a doctor, a plan her parents had been in full support of, and her interest in diagnostics had developed during med school when they were learning the different steps that led to a definitive diagnosis. The pieces fitted together like a puzzle, each new piece of information either confirming or ruling out a possible disease to the point where all answers had been assigned. Yara, who had perfect recall of every single thing she'd ever read in any textbook, excelled at solving those puzzles like no one else.

'I wanted to go into diagnostics, especially with how obscure the field still is. There is no formal training for it, and any physician who has a well-rounded background and is good at solving problems can become a diagnostician. My fellow practitioners and I are kind of self-styled in that sense.' She paused to chuckle, leaning into the warmth coming from Salvador's body. His hand on her stomach caused butterflies to stir inside it, making her shiver with every other circle he drew on her skin.

'I focused on general medicine, hoping to eventually find a way to focus on the diagnostic work of a hospital,' she continued, retelling a sequence of events only a few people around her knew. 'By the time I was done with my trainee years in practice, I was already married. My parents had arranged this blind date with the son of a business partner of theirs. He was a bio-medical engineer working for an up-and-coming start-up in the United States. We met a couple of times, with each subsequent date gaining more enthusiasm from both of our parents, and so…we ended up getting married after a short period of dating.'

So much of her self-worth as a woman had been tied up in her failing marriage that it had taken her years to realise how she had trapped herself in this loveless arrangement, and even longer to see how her parents had pushed her in this direction. Their approval had meant so much to her that she'd confused the infatuation with Lawrence for love and accepted his proposal, believing that her parents had her best interests in mind—not theirs, as it had turned out.

'I worked as a consultant for his company for a while, advising them on their market strategy for medical devices, which kept me in boardrooms and offices rather than in practices and hospitals. When they sold that company, Lawrence found a new position, but they already had their consulting staff on board, so I was left without a position.'

'He just left you out to dry when he found a new job?' His low voice was barely more than an incensed growl seeping through her pores and causing a shiver to trickle down her spine. The way he felt protective on her behalf, as if what she had been through was as outrageous as she perceived it from the inside, squeezed her heart so tightly she was sure it was going to burst. How could she have ever let anyone convince her that this man was not worthy of her? This decision would go down as one of the worst she'd ever made in her life.

'Turns out that kind of selfishness helped me establish my own career. I was able to use the connections I made during that time to get a few consulting gigs at actual hospitals, and when the opportunity to travel to different places to see patients came up, I jumped at it. Lawrence and I, we…' Her voice trailed off, and she noticed that Salvador's hand had stopped dead on her stomach as well. She sensed the ripple of tension going through his muscles, as if he was readying himself to come to her defence once more.

This was the painful part of her past, the details no one got to hear—not Bianca, not their mother, no one. Because even though she'd seen Lawrence for who he was ages ago—a self-centred opportunist more interested in her parents' money than being a real husband—she had stayed, because she was too ashamed to admit that she had made a mistake. That she had made many mistakes because she had a blind belief in the people who had raised her, not seeing that they were far more concerned with their family legacy and what people from the outside would see when they peered at it.

It was the reason why they had opposed her girlhood relationship with Salvador—there was no way of softening his family history and the trouble they had been through. It didn't matter to them that he was nothing like that. All they had cared about were the optics—just the same with her marriage. Her feelings for him had been irrelevant from the very start.

'We weren't happy for very long. I got married to him because I thought that was what my parents expected from me, and he proposed because he saw me as some sort of golden goose who would bring my parents' money with me into his start-up.' Admitting to her own blindness like that stung all over, and Yara squeezed her eyes shut to will the mounting humiliation away. 'I was so stupid to put so much trust into my parents, believing they were looking out for me.'

The tension she sensed building next to her snapped, and a moment later his other arm snaked around her, crushing her into his chest in an intimate hug. The surrounding noise faded away until it was just the two of them sitting on that plaid blanket in their own personal oasis of stillness and quiet.

His hands found her face, pulling it upward and towards him so he could plant a gentle kiss on her mouth, that tacit touch conveying so much more than words ever could.

'You're not dumb, unless you think I was dumb for thinking my parents would eventually change and see the error of their ways,' Salvador said when their lips finally came apart, peering deep into her eyes.

'What? No, of course not. How could you not believe that things would get better?'

'See? Of course, you would believe the best of the people who are meant to love you.' His words were gentle, caressing her in a deep part of her battered soul that yearned for just a bit of acknowledgement and care—things Salvador had been giving her over the last few days with such generosity and abundance that a part of her was afraid to leave. What would happen if she reached out and grabbed him tight enough so he couldn't slip away from her and do to her what she had done to him? The thought wormed itself into her brain, nestling into her until Salvador became all she could think about. But she knew she would be selfish to try. Yara had been the one to insist that whatever happened this weekend would only be for the duration of those two days. She had a life to get back to, and he had his nephew to take care of.

But weren't those things that they could do together? There was only one way to find out, and even though she now knew they were not only compatible as friends but also as lovers, her heart quaked at the thought of rejection, fearing the damage it would do to her already broken self. After all, it was her, once again, changing the rules and deciding that their relationship needed to change.

'Thank you, Salvador,' she whispered, her

face nestled into the crook of his neck so he couldn't see the pain in her expression. 'I've carried this weight with me for a long time, not knowing how to deal with it.'

His throaty chuckle drifted down to her ears. 'The Yara I know would seek to blame herself before seeking it in others. You're too kind to think anyone might have impure motives, and even though you might get hurt some more, I hope you won't let anyone change that about you. It's a good thing to have as a person.'

His right hand rubbed up and down her back while the left one came up to her face. Nimble fingers traced the line of her jaw until they reached her chin, lifting it up once more to meet his eyes. The dark intensity she had got to know over the last few days was gone, replaced by a warmth and deep affection that took all the air out of her lungs, forcing her to swallow the gasp growing in her throat. It was how he had used to look at her as a teenager. The lines around his mouth and eyes were new, so was the occasional grey streaking over his temples, but the glow was the same—and in that moment Yara fell over that cliff for him, diving into the depth of feelings she hadn't dared to thirty years ago.

Maybe there was a chance for them, if she was brave enough to reach out and grab it.

'Salvador…' The words caught in her throat, and loud laughter interrupted her thoughts as a group of people walked by them, each person seemingly talking over the others.

Maybe he'd sensed what she was about to confess, or maybe Yara was reading too much into the situation, wanting to ascribe meaning to something that was no more than a whim. But before she could find the courage to pick up her thoughts again, Salvador shifted underneath her and brought some space between them.

'Let's have a walk around the lake. If you remember this angle well, just wait until you see the other side,' he said as he got to his feet.

Despite the daze her thoughts were in, Yara snorted. 'The other side? Salvador, I can see it from here. Lagoa Bonita is a tiny little bead of water. I can use my imagination to see the other angle.'

Salvador pulled her up from the blanket and hauled her into his arms, wrapping his arms around her for a heartbeat, each one enjoying the closeness of the other—and the knowledge passing through them that they had to enjoy it while it lasted.

They spent the way back to Brasília in comfortable silence, neither of them feeling the urge to fill the space between them with unnecessary words. Despite their time together having been brief, Yara was buzzing with energy and feeling alive for the first time in many years. It was as if she'd been living her life in a daze, just wandering from one escape to the next, always on the lookout for that missing piece she sensed in her soul without ever understanding what it was.

Until this weekend, when she finally understood that it was Salvador.

A thought that brought a nervous flutter to her stomach. She had sunk way too deep into their old relationship again, to the point where she didn't know how she was going to extract herself from it. They had made a deal when he invited her away for this weekend—no strings attached.

Now she had gone and changed the rules. Or

at the very least, she had changed her mind. Despite the obstacles and warnings she had put between her and him, Yara had fallen in love with Salvador. Though their teenage romance ended too soon, she now had the opportunity to fix it. There was no more parental influence, no one to stand in the way of what she wanted except for her.

'You went to see Bianca. Did you see your mother as well?' Salvador asked, hitting eerily close to the thoughts she had been chasing around in her mind.

'Ah…no. Though I will probably see her next weekend. Bianca is throwing a party for our cousin's engagement, and, as the Lopes matriarch, my mother needs to be there to be seen.' Magda Lopes was just over eighty at this point, but she still made it to every single social event involving her family.

Salvador tilted his head at her. 'You think it'll take you another week to diagnose Mr Orlay?'

'No, I believe the diagnosis will be finalised at the start of the week. There are three potential diseases, so now it's a matter of going over all the symptoms again and ruling them out until the last one remains.'

'But you'll stay until the weekend?' There was something about his tone that sent a spark flying across her skin, settling in the pit of her stomach.

Was it hope softening his voice? A longing for her to stay longer? Or was that her lonely mind clinging to something that wasn't actually there just because she had realised the extent of her feelings for Salvador?

'Yes, Bianca twisted my arm. Said she would haunt me wherever I went next if I don't spend some time with her before I leave. Plus, I haven't really had time to dig into my emails and see what cases have come my way, so I don't know where I'll be going next.'

A part of her had avoided looking for her next job, though she wasn't sure why. She was far into Mr Orlay's diagnosis, confident that when she saw him tomorrow she would be able to rule out two of the three potential diseases and confirm the diagnosis. Then she would have the rest of the week to make some calls and arrangements for her next trip—a part she usually looked forward to when finishing a case. Only this time the thought came with a bitter aftertaste. It meant leaving. Again. When they had just reconnected on such a deep level.

'I thought maybe you were avoiding Magda because of your divorce and I…' He stopped himself from continuing his sentence, earning him an inquisitive look from Yara.

He pulled the car to the side of the road, and she realised that they had arrived back in Brasília. To her right, the high-rise building her hotel was in grew into the sky, its glass front glistening in the setting sun.

'You what?' She tilted her head, looking at him, eyes fixed on his face as he kept staring straight ahead.

'I was going to offer you my support if you did want to speak to her. Not that having me with you would make any conversation with her easier, but maybe it would help you.'

Yara's lips fell open as she looked at Salvador and processed his words. Was there a faint flush covering his cheeks or was the dimming light of the sunset playing tricks on her eyes? Either way, the gesture was just as kind and thoughtful as he had shown himself to be over the last week—and beyond that during their time together as teens.

She was not ready to let him go.

'I have somewhat of an indecent proposal for you, Dr Martins,' she said after a moment of consideration. The weekend couldn't end here, not when she had so much more to tell him.

He turned his head to face her, his eyebrows arching up. 'And what would that be?' His voice dropped low when he said those words, leaving no doubt in her mind that he knew exactly what kind of proposal she was thinking of. One fuelled by passionate nights tangled in each other's arms.

'I'm staying here until the end of the week. So…if you had a mind to extending our one-weekend-only arrangement for the week…' She left the rest of the sentence unsaid and watched as Salvador's jaw tightened, his eyes dipping below her face and gliding over her body.

Then he opened the car door abruptly, getting out and circling around the car to open her door for her. Yara took his outstretched hand to get out herself, and a moment later Salvador's body was covering hers as he pressed her against the side of the car, the cool metal on her back a stark contrast to the heat seeping into her body at the places where he met her skin.

His eyes narrowed on her, hunger shining in them as he bent down to kiss her on the lips.

'I have to stay at my place tonight, but I'll see you tomorrow at the hospital,' he said, his voice barely concealing his need for her after no more than a brief kiss. 'And we can take it from there.'

He let go of her, standing up straight and reaching for the back door to retrieve her bag from the seat.

'Do you want to go to the party with me?' she asked on a whim, thinking about the offer he'd made when it came to speaking to her mother.

Facing the Lopes matriarch with the news of her divorce gave her more anxiety than she wanted to admit. What other forty-seven-year-old woman was fretful about seeing her own mother? Having Salvador beside her would set quite a few tongues wagging, but Yara found that after this weekend she didn't care any more. Salvador, who had every right to still be furious with her, had accepted her back in his life with a gentleness that was far beyond her expectations. While he needed time to get to know her again, he'd been open to her words and reasoning. Not like her parents, who had only ever judged her by their own standards rather than seeing her as herself. But Salvador had acknowledged her as her own person, even at her very worst, and even though she had hurt him so much he was standing in front of her now, offering his support when it came to facing her mother again.

If he could accept her the way she was, why was it such a monumental request for her mother? Shouldn't she be the one to stand by her daughter, no matter what?

Salvador may have touched on the feelings she kept locked away for many years, but in doing so he did more than just spark a flame inside her heart. He showed her how much time and effort she wasted trying to live up to unattainable standards.

Yara was done living her life the way other people thought appropriate.

Salvador paused, and she wondered what was going through his head. He'd be walking into the den of the people who had rejected him just because of who his parents were. Then he leaned in again, brushing a soft kiss against her temple. 'As long as I don't have to look at anyone's rashes or ingrown toenails.'

'What kind of parties does your extended family throw that this is something you're worried about?' Yara laughed.

'One where they make sure to take advantage of their physician cousin,' he replied with a wry smile that turned into a genuine one when she put a hand on his cheek.

'Thank you, Salvador. For this weekend, and for coming with me to wrangle my family.'

'I'll see you tomorrow at work, *fofinha*.' He kissed her again, a lot more softly and deliberately this time, as if she was precious cargo that couldn't withstand too much force. Then he waved at her with a knowing grin, circling the car again to his seat and driving off.

Yara touched her lips where the ghost of his kiss still lingered, her knees weak from the impact this man had on her.

One week. That was the length of time she had to find the courage to tell him how she felt about him again—or to decide to walk out of his life again, with no turning back.

Yara had one week to decide whether to risk it all for Salvador, or to leave again without ever fulfilling the promise of their blooming relationship.

CHAPTER TEN

'MR ORLAY HAS Guillain-Barré Syndrome.' The room went quiet as Yara announced Henrique Orlay's diagnosis with a finality that only a diagnostician of her calibre could voice. Guillain-Barré was an exceedingly rare autoimmune disease that affected so few people each year. Salvador himself had only heard about it when they had spoken about the results of the tests during a short coffee break.

Now she had the entire team of doctors working on the case assembled in a conference room to discuss the diagnosis and the next steps for the patient.

Chief Sakamoto was the first to speak. 'Guillain-Barré Syndrome... I don't think we've ever seen this disease in the hospital during my time as the Chief of Medicine,' he said, and the surrounding room rumbled in agreement. 'How did you get to the final diagnosis?'

Salvador let his gaze wander around the

room, looking at the assembled doctors and nurses to see slight scepticism in some of their faces while others showed relief at finally having an answer to what ailed the patient all of them had worked so closely with.

'Mostly through the process of elimination,' Yara said with a generous smile that hit him right in the gut, sending showers of warmth flying through his body.

The warm sensation mingled with the dread her impending departure caused to stir in him. Against his better judgement and all his rational thought warning him against letting them get too close, he'd grown attached to her over the last ten days in ways he had never anticipated—or he would have never participated in a weekend of carnal desire away from the rest of society.

Now that he put it in a different light, he couldn't believe that he had for even a second thought this was a good idea. Some other part of his body had taken over the thinking duties when that decision had been made.

'We first believed his symptoms—bilateral arm weakness—to be a result of his valve replacement. A connection anyone would have made, though the typical side-effect is usually isolated in the left arm.' She paused, looking around the room as some people murmured again. 'There were no tumours on Mr Orlay's scans, nothing to show any disruption where information from the brain might not be reaching the rest of his body.'

This time, her sparkling brown eyes met his as she gave him a short nod with just the hint of a smile. Enough for Salvador's stomach to drop at how much he *wanted* her—not just in his bed, but also in his professional life, diagnosing patients in his hospital. Their connection had transcended something as simple as sex, showing them how well they worked together—both when it came to diagnosing patients and in emergency situations.

Salvador didn't know what to make of the myriad conflicting emotions blossoming in his chest, making it hard to see and think. They had an agreement, after all, and he was not free to give more—not with how many problems he brought with his family.

Felix needed stability and continuity in his life to break out of the criminal cycle his father had modelled for him. It was up to Salvador to provide that environment, and it was always going to be at a cost. Though when he thought of the sacrifices he made for his family, he thought of both time and money.

Now Salvador had to make another, but he was unprepared for how much this one already stung. He wasn't sure if they even needed to have a conversation, was hoping deep down inside that he could avoid it. If he stood face to face with Yara and spoke about the kernel of love growing in his chest, he wasn't sure if he'd be able to walk away.

But she wasn't rooted to one place while he was—an obstacle that could only be overcome with another sacrifice. One he couldn't make. And he could never ask her to give up anything either.

How could he ask her to come into his world, knowing he would never fit into hers?

'So, with Dr Martins' help, we performed a nerve-conduction velocity test so we could map out exactly where the signal was getting lost.' He perked up when he heard his name from her lips, looking over at her with a veiled expression. The look of pure and light affection that she gave him hitched his pulse up a few paces.

How was he supposed to find the strength in him to go back to his life as if she'd never returned?

Yara pointed at the TV in the conference room, now showing the test results of the NCV they had performed. 'The F waves on the first test were in the abnormal range. We ran the test again today and the F waves are absent.'

One of the doctors raised her hand. 'Is a NCV test how you distinguished this from something like transverse myelitis? Because in the previous scans, there seemed to be an inflammation in the spinal cord.'

'Yes, that's right. One of the first things we did is perform a spinal tap to get a look at the spinal fluid, and from that alone Guillain-Barré can be misinterpreted as transverse myelitis or polio.' She paused to nod at the doctor, thanking her for her question. 'Polio, of course, hasn't been seen in Brazil since the eighties, and, since the patient doesn't travel, this was an easy one to rule out.'

The room gave their congenial acknowledgment and Salvador nodded his encouragement with a gentle smile tugging on the corner of his lips.

'With the nerve-conduction velocity test and the spinal tap pointing towards an autoimmune disease, the final days have been a matter of observing the patient to see if the weakness in his arms and legs remained consistent on both sides.' She paused, looking around the silent room. 'And that is how we ended up with Guillain-Barré Syndrome.'

The room broke out in hushed whispers as the involved physicians discussed the diagnosis, and the general sentiment among them was quite clear—they were impressed. Hell, Salvador was probably more impressed than any of them for reasons that went much further than he could explain to any of them.

Not only was she the *hottest* woman he'd ever known, but she was also generous, kind and so incredibly smart that she kept the staff of an entire hospital on their toes as she figured out what ailed their patient when none of them could. And she remained humble while doing so, taking the time to gather the entire team to share her thought process and to give them some closure as they wrapped up the case.

Yara was in a league of her own, and for a painful moment the old wound she'd inflicted on him popped back open, leaving him stunned. Of course, she had run away from him so many years ago. She was a once-in-a-lifetime genius, meant for such tremendous greatness that Salvador couldn't even comprehend where it might take her. There was no way she was ever going to waste her time with him, who'd had to raise himself because his parents were either in jail or off losing what little money they had on the next big scheme.

How could he ever be enough to such a woman when his life was so complicated and hard? How could he even *ask*?

'As for the next steps…' This was the part Yara hated. She'd spent a lot of time unravelling the diagnosis just for her to end it on a sad note. 'You all know there are no known cures for autoimmune diseases at this point in time. What we can do is medicate for the current symptoms and adjust the treatment plan as his disease progresses, and as new medications are approved. It's not all bad news, though. Mr Orlay may have to learn to live with this as best he can, but at least we were able to tell him what's wrong. In my experience that counts for a lot.'

The room stayed silent this time, and Yara knew that sentiment well. They were all highly competitive individuals and none of them liked to think they lost against an unbeatable foe— even though that was a reality she faced more than others with the work she had chosen.

Chief Sakamoto stood up from his chair. 'And that brings Dr Silvia's time here to an end. We appreciate your expertise and all you were able to teach us. Dr Xander will take over further treatments of Mr Orlay, so if you have any questions, please go and talk to him. Thank you for your time, everyone.'

The gathered physicians shuffled to their feet, threads of different conversations reaching her ears as she searched the faces for the familiar one she'd seen just a few moments ago. Her eyes lit up with instantaneous affection when she spotted him. With his shoulder leaning against the wall and his corded arms crossed in front of his chest, Salvador looked like a delicious piece of masculinity, and she had to fight the urge to walk over there and throw her arms around him in some kind of primal territorial move.

Because he wasn't *hers*. Not really. Not until

she found the courage in her to tell him that she wanted to be with him. *If* he wanted to be with her…

The additional week she'd given herself had gone by much quicker than she had anticipated, with only three more nights left. Salvador had come to her hotel room every night, always leaving after a couple of hours to get back to his home and to Felix.

Tomorrow was her cousin Flávia's engagement party, and the last night they had together. She had extended an invitation to Felix as well. There'd be lots of children his age to hang out with, so he wouldn't feel lonely among a bunch of adults. But Salvador had declined the invitation, not specifying why he didn't want to bring his nephew along—and it was that small part that had bothered Yara ever since.

Did he not want her to meet his nephew? Was that why he wasn't bringing him? The rational side of her brain could come up with a handful of other reasons why he wouldn't want to bring Felix along, but the emotional side, the one reacting to Salvador so fiercely, went into a blind panic at that specific thought. Because that meant he kept his heart out of their entire affair—unlike her, who had fallen again so hard that she didn't know what her life was supposed to look like without him.

Her heart dropped into her stomach when he shifted his gaze onto her, sending her one of his rare smiles as he pushed himself off the wall and made to come over, only to be interrupted by Chief Sakamoto.

'Dr Silvia, if you have a moment, I'd like to discuss something in my office.'

She hesitated a moment, her eyes still on Salvador, who in turn looked at the chief and finally shrugged.

'Of course, lead the way,' she said, and followed the man down the corridor and into an office that was a lot smaller and down-to-earth than she'd expected. It was smaller than any other senior-staff office she'd seen during her travels, which spoke volumes about Dr Sakamoto's priorities for his hospital.

'Great work on Mr Orlay. We were fortunate that you came in when you did. While we do have resources, Centro Médico Juliana Amala is still growing, and our neurology department is only beginning to form.' He pointed at the seat across his desk, and Yara sat down, accepting his praise.

This was another part of her assignments she didn't like—the debrief with the Chief of Medicine. One of two things was about to happen. He would feel the need to justify *why* his doctors weren't able to diagnose the patient. Something Yara really didn't care about. She didn't consult on those cases to be right. She did it because she had a gift, and she needed to use it to help people. But her intervention sometimes left teams feeling inferior, as if somehow they should have been able to do it on their own.

If that wasn't the reason Chief Sakamoto had asked her into the office, then he was about to make her an offer to be a permanent member of staff. An offer Yara always immediately batted away, no matter how much money or prestige or influence they offered her.

Because once upon a time she'd needed the freedom her career offered her. The less time she spent at home, the better—though that behaviour had led to her avoiding taking responsibility for her unhappiness in her relationship. Though Salvador was different, he was sweet and freeing, never forgetting what *she* wanted.

Would staying in one place be such a bad thing when he was who she was staying for?

'Now, I'm sure you get this everywhere you go, but I have to ask just on the off-chance that you might say yes. I think your talent and methods are incredible, Dr Silvia. What would it take to convince you to join my hospital?' Dr Sakamoto paused, his gaze fixed on her, and Yara hoped he couldn't see her pulse flutter at the base of her throat. 'With you at the helm we could become Brazil's number-one diagnostic centre, where people come with the most difficult cases.'

Yara leaned back in her chair, the usual immediate rejection clinging to her lips, not quite ready to pass the threshold.

The chief seemed to sense her hesitation as well, pouncing on the opportunity he saw open up in front of him. 'Name whatever you want, and we'll make it happen. I want to make this a good deal for you because you coming to work in my hospital will increase our influence across the country.'

There was nothing Chief Sakamoto could dangle in front of her—at least nothing that was his to give.

She wanted Salvador.

'Thank you for the offer, Dr Sakamoto. Let me think about this.'

When she walked back past the conference room, no one was in there any more. Yara frowned at the disappointment pooling in her stomach.

It wasn't as if she had anything to discuss with him—other than her life-altering feelings for him. That wasn't something she planned on discussing here. She needed some privacy for that—as well as courage to push through with actually speaking the words pounding against the walls of her chest.

I love you.

What was so hard about that?

CHAPTER ELEVEN

'*MINHA IRMÃ*…YOU need to sit down and have a drink,' Bianca said, placing a firm hand on her sister's arm and pulling her down onto one of the chairs placed on the pavement.

The council had agreed to close several local streets for the afternoon in return for a small donation and if the entire neighbourhood was allowed to attend—an offer her cousin Flávia happily accepted. As someone who enjoyed being the centre of attention, she couldn't have enough people at her engagement party.

There were many groups of people clustering together, and each time whispers went through them Yara craned her neck to see if Salvador's arrival was setting any tongues wagging.

She wished for a moment that they had established some ground rules for this party— even though they had a terrible track record of following those. Were they supposed to keep their distance? Or live as they did when it was just the two of them? It wasn't as if either of them had acted in a particularly secretive way around people. At work they kept their distance simply because that was the professional thing to do.

'What are you so worried about?' Bianca offered her a glass of caipirinha, which she took without registering, taking a small sip. The crushed lime perked up her senses as it slid down her throat, making her cough at the sudden acidity.

'I wasn't really planning on a great reunion between Salvador and Mum. Now that I'm putting these words out there, I actually think this is a truly terrible idea, and I don't know what came over me.'

Bianca frowned at her. 'It's been thirty years… I'm sure everyone has moved on from things.'

'Do we have the same mother?' The words came out with more bite than Yara anticipated, and she regretted her tone the second she heard her words.

How differently their parents had treated the sisters had been a topic of long discussions between tears and spilled wine. Because Bianca had come as a surprise to her parents almost ten years after their first daughter was born, she hadn't felt the weight of the Lopes legacy on her shoulders and had received a lot more leeway from their parents when it came to both her career and the fact that she chose to love herself first and foremost.

Yara was glad her sister was spared the scrutiny of both their parents, being able to develop her life in the way she wanted to.

'I'm sorry… I'm just nervous. You know she doesn't know about the…divorce.' The word still felt weird on her lips. From the very crib, Yara had been raised as an overachiever. Divorce sounded so much like giving up, even though she couldn't be happier to finally be free of that loveless relationship.

Now she only needed to somehow broach the topic with her mother.

'It's so silly how much this is making me sweat. I'm forty-seven! An accomplished doctor, well respected in her field.'

'Oh, are we bragging about our titles now?' Both Yara and Bianca whipped their heads around when that deep voice cut through the crowd. The low bass seeped through Yara's pores, nestling itself into the area behind her navel, where it promptly lit a roaring fire to pump heat through her entire body.

'Salvador, you made it.' Yara jumped to her feet, taking the three steps that separated him from where the sisters were sitting. 'I was looking around for you.'

'Rosalinda and her son saw me, so I stopped to catch up with them. Do you remember her house?' He looked around, pointing at a building a couple of streets down with a sky-blue fence around the garden.

Yara laughed when she followed his pointing finger. 'Didn't she have mango trees in her garden?'

'Yep, and she knew exactly who was responsible for her missing fruit. She just demanded ten real from me.'

'Ten? Her mangoes were nice, but that is daylight robbery. You didn't give it to her, did you?'

Salvador shrugged, a smile playing on his lips. 'I had to. She had her cane with her, and I'm still scared of her.'

Yara laughed, picturing him being chased

by old Rosalinda and her cane. Though Salvador had been from a completely different background to her, her neighbours and relatives had soon come to know the boy hanging out at the Lopes' house. Some had been warm and welcoming like Rosalinda, who had never cared where he came from, only how he treated Yara. Others, though, had leaned more in the direction of her own mother, condemning his character before they could get to know him just because of his parents.

The whispers they heard today were much quieter from the latter people.

Nevertheless, a smile stayed on her lips as she looked at him, affection running so deep in her veins that she wanted to throw her arms around him. But was that the kind of relationship they were having in public? They hadn't even mentioned it when she invited him to the engagement party. His role was supposed to be around emotional support as Yara faced her mother for the first time in many years. Would he want to do that from the back row, or right by her side while holding her hand?

Holding hands in public didn't seem very no-strings-attached, but then again, nothing about their affair so far spelled anything remotely casual.

The air around them grew tense. Yara's smile froze in place as she kept staring at him, unsure how to react or how she should move on from the conversation. How was she supposed to act around him? That question sent her brain into a tailspin, unable to decide.

That was when Salvador stepped forward, dragging his knuckles over her cheek in an affectionate gesture, and lowered his lips to hers, brushing over them in the hint of a kiss before he straightened up again. His gaze was fixed on someone behind her, and when Yara whirled around to look at her sister he slid his hand into hers, their fingers intertwined.

Her heart leapt into her mouth when their skin touched. Her mind was falling from one spiral to the next, now solely focused on where his hand was touching hers and what that meant for them. Was this a grand declaration in front of her old friends and neighbours? Or was this just part of that *thing* they had agreed on—and it didn't mean as much as she would like it to mean?

Or…was it possible that he felt the same way?

Today was the day of her deadline. Either she told him, or she would for ever lose the chance at a future with Salvador.

'Bianca, good to see you again.' Salvador stepped towards the chair where her sister sat.

'Likewise. I'm surprised how many people still know your face around here when you lived on the other side of town.'

Salvador barked a gruff laugh. 'We spent a lot of time roaming outside to avoid the glares and verbal jabs from your parents. They were bound to notice that strange boy hanging around the Lopes offspring.'

'Oh, I remember other things…' Bianca wiggled her eyebrows up and down, giving Yara the signal that she'd spent enough time around her sister with the man she was hopelessly in love with. If she stayed here any longer, those caipirinhas might make her reveal more than was appropriate.

'Do you want to do the rounds and say hi to people? Flávia is somewhere over there, getting counsel from the neighbourhood elders on how to create a successful marriage.' She waved her hand to the other end of street, where a large crowd had gathered around some tables that had been brought outside from various houses.

'That sounds like interesting advice.'

'It does?' Yara raised a sceptical eyebrow at him.

Salvador pulled her a few steps forward, nodding at people as they recognised them. 'You don't want to learn how people built their lasting marriages?'

A cynical snort left her nose, the bitterness she felt still so raw that its intensity surprised her. 'The way to have a lasting marriage is not getting married in the first place. I learned my lesson with that.'

They stopped on the pavement, Salvador's gaze gliding over the people surrounding them before he looked at her. The friendly spark she'd seen in his eyes as he had approached her was gone, replaced by a thick veil that wouldn't let her read what lay beyond it. His expression became closed off.

'You don't want to get married again?' His voice sounded strangely distant and in an instant Yara saw all her plans slip through her fingers. Was that what he wanted from her?

Marriage? When he knew how broken the last one had left her?

To give someone that kind of sway and control over her again would take so much out of her. She wasn't sure she was free to give this piece of her to anyone any more. Not even to Salvador, the man who had bypassed all the barriers she'd put up around her heart, as if he'd always been in there, just waiting for her to be ready.

But a second marriage? The concept struck unprecedented fear in her heart, making her recoil from the thought of ever signing a marriage certificate again.

'I've been through this before, and it didn't work out. When I needed to get out for my own sanity, it made things so much harder to unravel when I just needed to be gone.' Lawrence had not made things easy on her, holding her to promises she had made out of obligation to her family, thinking that her infatuation for this man was true love.

'What about—?'

'*Minha filha*—it's really you!'

The blood froze in her veins when the voice of her mother drifted towards her, rendering her immobile and unable to act for a few seconds. Salvador's arm came around her hip as he sensed her tense up, enveloping her with his warmth to lend her whatever strength she needed.

'*Mãe... Oi...*' she said as she turned around to face the encounter she'd been dreading the moment she set foot in Brasília.

'*Filhota*, I'm so glad to see you...' Magda Lopes' voice trailed off as she stepped closer, her milky eyes scanning the man whose arm was draped around her daughter's waist, holding her close to his body. 'That's not—'

'Mama, I'm sure you remember Salvador? He used to hang out at our house a lot when we were at school together.' Yara had to admit that although she was a meticulous planner, she had not at all thought about what would happen if her mother saw her snuggled in Salvador's arms.

The perplexed look on her mother's face gave her a strange sense of vindication that she didn't want to examine too closely.

'Of course. How could I forget?' Her note was teetering between friendly and disapproving, these two polarities tightly wrapped into a pinched smile that lacked any warmth. 'I guess, then, I shouldn't ask about your husband. I mean, you've already shown all the neighbours—'

'Ex-husband, Mãe. After many years of not even living on the same continent any more, I thought it was time to finally rectify the mistake I made when I agreed to marry him. A mistake that you and Dad pushed me into for your own selfish reasons.' A dam deep down within her broke when she said those words, the beginning of catharsis, and she finally came clean about the things she'd carried on her shoulders so long.

'I'm sorry? You cannot be serious. Your father and I always had your best interests in mind.' Her mother grabbed at the thin silken shawl wrapped around her neck, an indignant look on her face.

'Please spare me the lecture. You want to tell me you had my best interests in mind when you threatened to withhold my tuition if I didn't stop talking to Salvador? You saw Salvador and me getting closer, and you were worried what Dad's friends at the yacht club would say about the questionable upbringing of my boyfriend.

If you had never interfered, if my happiness had not come second to your desire to keep the family name in pristine condition, maybe I would have ended up marrying this man that I was supposed to be with, saving me years of unhappiness that I've only now started to claw back.'

The words flowed over her lips without restraint as the final walls around her hurt soul came down, and she had once again Salvador to thank for it. He showed her that she was good enough with his acceptance of her, despite all of the mistakes she'd made. The burden of her own guilt lifted, making her feel lighter than she had in years. So light that she hadn't noticed Salvador tense up beside her as she spoke.

Under any other circumstances, Salvador would have excused himself a couple of sentences ago to let Yara and her mother deal with their tension in their own time. But he knew how much Yara had worried about that moment—and none of that concern was wasted from where he was looking at it.

He was also in the unique position where the argument involved him as well. Though he knew her parents had interfered in their relationship, he hadn't realised how far they had gone to stop them from being together. They had truly gone to the lengths of withholding her tuition money, threatening her placement at med school? He couldn't even be angry at her any more, knowing the truth. This was an impossible decision to make.

But the ringing in his ears didn't come from the piercing look Magda Lopes hurled his way. No, the rushing sensation was due to the words Yara had said, that snippet replaying in his head over and over again, until the words lost all meaning.

I would have ended up marrying this man that I was supposed to be with. Him.

Yara believed they would still be together without her parents' undue influence over her.

Confusion stirred its cold fingers in the pit of his stomach, mingling with the heat her blurted confession summoned to his body, bringing forth a storm that roiled through his insides. Her stalwart resolve that they would still be together touched him in an unexpected way. How would their relationship have changed once he started to notice his same-sex attraction? Or was he overthinking this, finding problems where there were none?

When he'd brought up marriage, he hadn't thought much of it. Nor when he'd decided to kiss her in front of her old neighbourhood. It had just felt right, as though being with this woman was what he was supposed to do with his life.

They weren't supposed to talk as if these things were for *them*. It didn't matter that Yara was too hurt from her previous marriage because he wasn't about to propose. They weren't a couple, no matter how easy it felt to hold her hand and walk among neighbours as if they were. But she didn't want to commit to a relationship like that, while Salvador couldn't do without it.

Except now Yara was standing next to him proclaiming to her mother that they were meant to be—and still would be if her parents hadn't interfered.

The two concepts warred in his chest, pulling him in different directions as he struggled to reconcile her feelings for him with her fear of giving someone so much of her. How could both be real?

'Yara, if you could come over and we can talk just between us,' Magda said with a pointed glare at him. The conversation had moved on without him when the turmoil within him had broken loose at her words.

'I'm done having conversations with you.' Yara's hand tightened around his, squeezing it with the trepidation that must have been rising within her. His protective instincts kicked in and his arm looped tighter around her waist, drawing her closer, even though the proximity was tearing at his heart.

'This is Flávia's engagement party, and we're not having this discussion here when we should be celebrating. If you want to talk I'm open to it, but only if you accept my decisions.'

Magda's complexion lost all colour as she stared at her daughter with a surprised expression. 'Is that how it is? Don't think I will stand here and watch you make terrible life choices.'

'Good thing you won't be invited to my engagement party when it happens,' Yara retorted.

All the insecurity and fragility about this moment floated to the surface, and he wanted nothing more than to pull her into his arms, to kiss the tension away. But Salvador was frozen himself, unable to put his own turmoil aside. Uncertainty was something he didn't deal with very well, leaving his nerves frayed.

'Let's go,' Yara mumbled, drawing him away until they were surrounded by people.

They stayed silent as they wove through the crowd, their only connection their clasped hands. Every now and then someone stopped them to talk to either Yara or Salvador, some of them smiling with genuine joy that the two had finally got together, showing them a version of the future they couldn't have.

This moment was only one of many sacrifices he had to make to keep Felix safe—though none had hurt as much as his heart compressing in his chest right now. Walking around the neighbourhood, chatting to people and slowly pulling Yara out of her gloomy mood, had shown him a window into a life he couldn't have, even though every fibre in his body yearned for it.

How had he fallen in love with Yara again?

'I didn't realise how much they had manipulated you,' he said, when they moved on from a group of people asking them about their work in the hospital.

Yara had gone into details about her travels and some of the rarer conditions she helped diagnose in different countries. Her face lit up when she spoke about it, twisting the long and thin knife deeper through his ribs, stealing the remaining air in his lungs. He'd fallen in love with this woman when their lives couldn't be more different.

'I didn't want to talk about it, though now I'm not sure why. I guess I felt insecure about it. Like, what would you think of me if you knew how weak I had been, choosing my tuition over you?' she said, with a thin laugh.

'They forced you to choose your future over some boy you liked. I can understand your choice. Hell, if you had told me about it back then, *I* would have made that choice for you.' Salvador pulled her closer, a need to protect her surging as the other half of his brain told him that he needed to stop right this moment. He *couldn't* be her protector, not when he already had someone else to look out for.

But her words were stuck in his brain, playing on repeat as he struggled to reconcile what she had said with what they were doing.

I would have ended up marrying this man that I was supposed to be with.

'Yara…' He stopped in his tracks to face her and the deep breath she took when their eyes met told him everything he needed to know— that this hadn't just been a throwaway comment, and she knew he was going to ask about it now.

The buzzing of his phone interrupted them, and he slipped it out of his pocket. 'Oh, it's the babysitter. I have to get that.'

He pressed the green answer button, holding the phone to his ear. 'Hey, Ciara, what's up?'

For the second time today, everything around him went quiet as the blood rushed to his ears. 'What happened?'

Yara looked at the chest X-rays, a deep line between her brows, before turning back to Salvador, who was nervously pacing up and down the empty examination room they had retreated into when Felix's films had arrived. She still wasn't clear on what exactly had happened, only that she was looking at a broken rib and a potential pneumothorax.

Salvador had huffed at the diagnosis of the

on-duty physician, pushing a tablet with Felix's medical history and the report from the paramedics into her hands. She had thrown an apologetic look towards the doctor, who didn't seem to mind as much as she would have.

'I'll take one more doctor, I don't care about the consequences,' he'd said, and left them with the care of Felix.

She put a hand on Salvador's arm to stop him from pacing. 'It's okay. Nothing too bad has happened. Once I know what the lung sounds like, I'll page someone from Paediatrics to place the chest tube. A few days of rest and he'll be as good as new.'

His features darkened, worry mingling with something much more menacing as he drew a sharp breath. 'Nothing too bad happened. Ciara told me the police came by my apartment to inform her that Felix had sneaked out of his room to meet up with some friends. They were found on someone else's property trying to *break in*.'

Her eyes widened at the unveiled terror now surfacing in Salvador's features. She wasn't quite scared, but the distress etched into his gaze made her feel off kilter. 'I think we need to focus on his health—'

'And you know where I was while he was off hanging out with the wrong crowd? I was at that party, playing pretend marriage with someone who will never commit to me in this way. I let myself be distracted when I really needed to be paying attention to Felix.'

He moved his arm away from her hand—now hovering aimlessly in the air—and turned his back towards her. Tension rippled through his muscles, his hands flexing by his sides as he stepped away while taking deep breaths.

Yara blinked as she stared at an invisible point between his shoulder blades. Hurt bloomed in her chest, driving the air out of her lungs and leaving her empty, struggling. *Playing pretend marriage?* Was that how he felt about their time together? As if the deep affection filling the place between them was nothing more than a game they had indulged in for far too long?

A distraction? The room around Yara turned wobbly and strange, her legs not really knowing where they could stand without losing equilibrium. His words drove a searing spear into her chest, cracking her open with a wound so great, her vision blurred as tears pricked her eyes.

She wiped them away with the sleeve of her

lab coat, squeezing them shut and forcing herself to remember how to breathe. Salvador was scared and cornered. Something terrible had just happened to his nephew, the boy who had become like his son. Hurt people lashed out, striking at the first thing they could control—whether deserved or not didn't matter. Right now, he wasn't a doctor working in this hospital, but the visitor of a loved one who needed her full attention.

Gathering the paper-thin resolve she had clawed together from the distant corners of her mind, she straightened her posture. 'Parents are not allowed in the emergency department, Salvador. Go and wait in the paediatric wing. I'll have them page you once he's ready to be transferred.'

She didn't wait for his reply before stepping out of the room and into the patient room where Felix was lying in a bed, his expression one of pain, but otherwise alert.

'Hi, Felix. I'm Yara, and I work here with your uncle,' she said, putting on her best patient-care smile as she shoved the encounter with Salvador far down behind her mental shields. 'How are you feeling?'

'Bad…'

She had to chuckle at the straightforward answer. Salvador and his nephew were alike in that regard. When she noticed that he was craning his neck to look at her, she fetched a stool from the far end of the room and sat down at his bedside.

'Can you tell me what happened? The paramedics told me they think you slipped and fell.' She didn't mean to pry any details out of him, but rather cover all angles of his diagnosis, since she didn't know the circumstances that had led to his fall. Had they been having a fight? Had he hit his head, maybe?

Felix stared at her with apprehension, his dark eyes the same shade as Salvador's. A stray strand of anxiety broke free from the tight cage she had put on anything relating to him and she squashed it down with more effort than expected.

'Are you…the woman Tio has been seeing this week?' he asked after a moment of consideration.

Yara's eyebrows rose, almost vanishing into her hairline. How could he have possibly guessed that? She shot a quick glance over her shoulder to check her surroundings. Had he been able to see them arguing just a few moments ago? But though there was a window in the patient room, the blinds were drawn, so he couldn't have seen them.

What was she supposed to say to that? She furrowed her brow, then quickly decided on the truth. The boy was astute and observant enough to notice what his uncle had been up to the last two weeks, so he deserved at least some parts of the truth.

'Yes, that's me. I've known your *tio* since we went to school together.' His expression became closed off, and Yara reached out her hand as if to stop it from happening. 'But don't worry about how I know him. I'm your doctor, so I'm not allowed to share anything with your uncle unless you give me permission to do so.'

'Really?'

Yara nodded. 'Yep. It's called doctor-patient confidentiality. I might share important information with your guardian only to the extent that is necessary to inform your treatment. But your *tio* won't be involved in any procedure since he is your legal guardian.'

A pained expression fluttered over Felix's

face at the mention of the guardianship, too quick for her to read it. Guilt? Or was it just the discomfort of his injuries?

'My...friends wanted to go to this fancy house. There was a big party near by, so they figured it would be empty. They boosted me over the wall since I'm the strongest and I could lift them over, but then I lost my footing and fell down the wall.'

Yara nodded, her expression schooled into professional detachment. 'How did you land? On your head? On your side?'

'On my stomach,' he replied, now looking down at his hands.

'I see. Well, that's mostly good news, then. You have a cracked rib and a part of your lung collapsed—which is not even half as scary as it sounds. It just means there is a bit of free air in your chest cavity that we need to remove. But we'll call a specialist from Paediatrics for that.'

His breath left his nose in short bursts. Yara reached out when she saw tears form in his eyes. 'I'm really sorry. I know this was stupid. I didn't know that this was why the boys had invited me to come along with them until we were there.' Felix's chest started to heave as he gulped down air, the weight of his own conscience becoming too much for him to bear. 'Tio is going to be so mad.'

'It's okay, Felix. That's not something we need to worry about right now.' She got off the chair and sat on the bed instead, taking his hand in hers and squeezing it with a reassuring smile. 'First, we want to get you back on your feet, and I promise you, the only thing your *tio* is worried about right now is your wellbeing.'

The boy calmed down, nodding at her with a small sob that wrenched at her heart. She could see Salvador's influence in the way Felix spoke, worried about disappointing his uncle by doing something forbidden.

'So, here's what we're going to do. I'm going to find someone to transport you to your room, where a doctor will explain the next steps in your treatment to you. You'll definitely need to stay here overnight for observation, but that's something we'll all discuss together with you and your *tio*.'

Felix nodded, swiping at the tears forming in his eyes and biting his lip anxiously.

'Anything else you want to ask me before I go?'

Some of the tension in his face faded and his mouth opened, a question on the tip of his tongue. 'Are you Tio's girlfriend?'

Yara blinked several times at the question. That was not what she had expected when she asked him if he wanted to know anything else. 'Um… No, I'm not.'

The hot blade that had slowly been forcing its way up between her ribs plunged deeper at her words, and she bit the inside of her cheek so as not to wince.

'Maybe you should be. Uncle Salvador has been a lot happier in the last two weeks, and you're the only thing that changed for him.'

Her heart slammed against her chest, wiggling at the blade still stuck in her ribs, and rippling a profound and tremendous pain through her body that almost made her gasp out loud. She quickly got up from the bed, turning around and dabbing at her eyes again, struggling to keep her composure.

When she had finally put her face on again, she turned around to smile at Salvador's nephew. 'That'll be nothing compared to how happy he'll be to see you once you're all patched up,' she said, the smile not quite reaching her eyes as she reached out and patted the boy's hand one last time before leaving the room.

His words echoed in her head. He'd given her a piece of information she had been missing. One that stood in direct contrast with what Salvador had barked at her just a few moments ago. But he was in distress, worried sick about his nephew. She would be foolish to let his words carry too much weight.

Salvador being happier than his nephew had ever seen him meant he might feel the same way about her, after all. But she needed to tell him—now.

While Yara went to check on Felix, Salvador did as she had asked him to and went up to the paediatric department, where he sat down in the waiting area for only a few minutes before the nervous energy took over and he started pacing the corridors, only curtly nodding at the colleagues that recognised him from Radiology.

After the paediatrician had placed the chest tube, Salvador had finally been able to step into the room, hugging his nephew as tightly as he could with a broken rib. By the time his doctor had gone over the next steps, Salvador could see the pain medication kicking in, for Felix could barely keep his eyes open.

There were two tracks playing in his mind concurrently—what Ciara had heard about Felix's accident, and the conversation he'd had with Yara not even an hour ago.

His heart was sick with grief and worry for his nephew, thinking he'd somehow failed him and that Felix was already walking a dangerous path where Salvador couldn't reach him. He'd given everything he had—*everything*—to keep Felix from tumbling, building safety nets and securities along the way to catch him whenever he strayed. He had even given up on dating, believing that all his attention should be on his nephew and raising him to be a good person.

Then Yara had dropped back into his life, upending it without even meaning to. She had arrived and suddenly the world was in colour again when it had been sepia for so damn long. He'd fallen the moment he spoke to her again, realising that the hole in his chest was left there when she had disappeared from his life—and only she could fix it.

Yara. The one who'd got away.

He'd been so eager to lose himself in that tantalising ancient love that he'd become complacent in other parts of his life. He'd stopped paying so much attention to Felix, choosing to spend his evenings with Yara rather than at home, watching over the boy. It was *his* fault that this had happened today—and, though Salvador's heart was breaking, he had to make sure he was never so careless again.

Yara hadn't come up with them after she handed the case over to the paediatric consultant. Was she still in the hospital? He fished his phone out of his pocket to check his messages, but she hadn't contacted him. Maybe his unkind outburst had been enough to drive her away.

Salvador shivered as he remembered, the truth of his hesitation to commit laid bare. The pain and anger he carried within him had festered into something tainted inside, that ugly insecurity rearing its head the second he was pressed into a corner. In his mind he knew the difficult situation Yara had been in. Her parents had threatened her future, and with that, her entire life.

But the knowledge of that didn't change the

fact that the wound in his heart still bled, ripped open by her sudden presence in his life. Salvador had spent years on his own as the quiet voice in his head whispered words of caution and betrayal. A result of the deep hurt that had never healed. How could he trust her to be in his life—to be in Felix's life—when the faintest amount of pressure made him close off and retreat?

Feeling the weight of this day bear down on his shoulders, Salvador sighed and let himself drop into one of the chairs in the waiting area, burying his face in his hand.

The soft crinkle of plastic pulled him out of his contemplations. Yara sat next to him and held out her hand.

'Crisps?'

'We didn't eat when we were at the engagement party. I know I can't convince you to go home and sleep, so you have to eat whatever the vending machine has to offer.' She shook the bag of crisps at him until he grabbed it from her, turning the package around in his hands as the tension rippled through the air between them.

'Thanks for looking after him,' he said when he couldn't stand the silence any more.

258 FALLING AGAIN FOR THE BRAZILIAN DOC

'Of course, least I could do...' She hesitated, her open hand hovering in the air between them before she closed it into a fist. 'He's going to be fine. The chest tube is already out. Some sleep and night-time observation to ensure he doesn't have concussion, then he can go straight back home.'

'That's not what I'm worried about,' Salvador mumbled, his head falling back into his open palm, rubbing the weariness out of his eyes.

'I don't know how much my opinion matters to you at this point, but I think he just made a mistake—like you did when you were twelve.' The way she paused in between her words, selecting them with care and intention—it was so unlike the way Yara spoke to him that he looked up. His brow knotted as he scrutinised her.

Of course, his earlier outburst had affected her. He would have been a fool to believe otherwise. Maybe this was his chance to let her go, end it once and for all. They weren't going to work out, not with so many obstacles already in their way.

'He wouldn't be in this hospital right now if I had paid better attention to him,' he said, the fear-fuelled fire in his stomach roaring back to life.

'Maybe. Or maybe he would have. He sneaked out of the house. If the babysitter didn't know, you wouldn't have, either.'

'But I would have known who the boys are. I would have known who he's hanging out with. If I hadn't been distracted...' He stopped himself before he could finish the sentence, but the damage was already done.

Yara leaned back, and the mist in her eyes made him hate himself. Why had he let it go so far? Why had he agreed to this in the first place, when she was the one person who knew how to get under his skin? From the very beginning, they'd trodden a perilous path and were now surprised that they had broken each other.

'Please...finish that sentence.' Her voice was thick, and she blinked several times, wiping the gloss from her eyes.

'Yara, I'm sorry. I think we...maybe we let ourselves be carried away by this little affair.' Salvador dared to reach out but withdrew his hand when she flinched away from him.

'This little...? That's how you think about what's happened between us? And here I thought…' She got off her chair, turning her back to him and tilting her head up to look at the ceiling. Her shoulders rose and fell with every big breath, and he felt each breath in his own chest—each one getting harder to get down as the air between them thickened.

This was it. Their final moment.

'I thought you loved me too. Because that's what I came here to say. That I love you, and I didn't care about what you said earlier,' she finally said, and even though the words had lived in his head since he'd pulled her to him the first time they'd slept together at his house in Planaltina, they thundered through him, searing his very soul.

The words burned on his lips, the urge to say them back to her tearing through him. There she was, the woman he'd desired for so many years, telling him she loved him—with such pain in her expression that he almost caved in on himself.

'Yara, I…' The rest of the sentence refused to pass his lips. Because where would that leave them? She was going tomorrow, and he had his nephew to take care of, the worry for him so strong that he had lashed out at her the moment the pressure became too much.

He had, once again, shown himself to be unworthy of her—unable to ever bridge the gap between them.

'I will not stand here and let you tell me that I was only a *distraction*—that this meant nothing to you, when I know what I sensed between us.' A fire had entered her eyes, burning with an indomitable spirit that he had nothing but admiration for. In a different life, he would have been the fuel for that fire.

'We both agreed what this would be. The rules—'

Yara didn't let him finish his sentence. 'Screw the rules! Just for one moment, humour me and do not hide behind technicalities, Salvador. I know I messed up thirty years ago. I know it now. Hell, I even knew it back then. Now I'm scarred and hurt, but I want to try. For you. For us.'

'Enough that you would marry me?' The words flew out of his mouth before he could stop himself, hitting at the heart of his insecurities with Yara—that he wouldn't survive if she left him again.

'Are you…? I… Is this a…proposal?' She whispered the last word, her eyes so wide he could see the sliver of white surrounding them.

'Would you accept?' He stood now, too deep into this to back out. He never wanted to ask her to give up anything in her life, but she spoke about *us* when they were at such different points in their lives.

'I… Salvador, I can't.' Her chest fluttered with every breath.

'Me neither.' He shook his head, his heart cracking. They were so close to figuring it all out, but the more he looked at it, the further they drifted away. 'I have Felix to look out for now. I just can't be involved with someone who won't stick around when it counts.'

Shock widened her eyes when he said those words, and he noticed her slight recoil. Her mouth opened and closed several times before she finally cleared her throat, once again blinking rapidly.

'So, it comes back to this. You don't trust me because I left.' Bitterness laced her words. 'I made a mistake, Salvador. And even though you now know the truth of how my decision came about, I still own it.'

The sight of her pain was almost too much to bear. Each breath closed his chest tighter until his heart burst into tiny fragments.

'You had to do right by your family back then. I have to do the same now. Felix has had enough turmoil to last a lifetime. I don't mean to add more to it.' The finality in his tone settled in between them, bearing down on the silence spreading in the room that only their breaths interrupted.

Yara took a step towards him, the spark in her eyes gone and the deep hurt etched into her features, summoning his protectiveness forward— but how could he protect her from himself?

'I should go... I still haven't congratulated Flávia on her engagement.' It was a flimsy excuse to leave, probably the first thing that had entered her mind when she searched for an elegant exit, but Salvador nodded.

'It's only been a few hours. I'm sure they'll be going all night.'

'I... Yes, okay... I'd better leave then. *Tchau*, Salvador.'

Their eyes met for what he knew to be the last time, and he looked deep into them, creating a mental image of the small constellation in her eyes for him to keep. He wanted to re-member her—if they couldn't be together, at least he'd have that.

'Tchau, fofa.'

Yara took a step back, then another, until she finally turned on her heel and walked around the counter and out of sight. When he couldn't hear her footsteps any more, Salvador broke apart, falling back on the chair he'd been sit-ting on. Pain shot through his body as if he'd been sliced open from one side to the other, exposing everything weak and vulnerable for whoever looked close enough.

Somehow, it hurt even worse than it had thirty years ago, leaving him empty and hol-low. The space inside his chest, the one she had occupied with such confidence and space, lay bare again, its edges burning with an acute awareness of what was missing.

The ultimate sacrifice—to keep his focus trained on Felix. No matter what the personal cost.

CHAPTER TWELVE

AFTER THE FIRST night Felix showed some signs of a traumatic head injury, so the paediatric specialist treating him decided it would be best to keep him in the hospital for a few more days, just to be on the safe side—something Salvador was a lot happier about than his nephew. Having him stay at the hospital meant he'd be able to work while also keeping an eye on him.

And work was the only thing keeping his mind off his wretched experience ever since Yara had left—again. Though this time it was because he couldn't let her back into his life. Pushing her away had taken every shred of strength in his body, and even now, days later, he was wracked by guilt and doubt, one foot always ready to run back to her.

Though she was gone, probably already in a new country working on a case no one else could solve.

His phone buzzed, and he looked down from

his screen, where he'd been deconstructing a complex full-body scan to understand what they were looking at. The charge nurse from the paediatric department was paging him, prompting him to furrow his brow.

When he'd gone there to check on Felix that morning, they'd told him he would be discharged in the evening so Salvador could take him home. Had they pulled the discharge forward because they needed the bed?

'I'll be right back,' he said to his colleague, sitting next to him at a different computer, and headed to the nurses' desk in Paediatrics.

The nurse guided him towards Felix's room, and only her nonchalant and unhurried demeanour kept the panic for his nephew's safety at bay. If something had happened, he would sense it in the way they treated him, wouldn't he?

When he stepped into the room, Chief Sakamoto was sitting on a chair next to Felix's bed, playing a game of cards with the boy. Both looked up when Salvador entered.

'Ah, Dr Martins. Come over here and sit down.' The man waved at a chair next to him, and a different alert went off in the back of Salvador's mind. Why was the Chief of Medicine playing cards with his nephew? He and Salvador were not close enough for this to be normal.

'What's going on here?' He paused, looking at each of them with narrowed eyes. 'Is this some kind of intervention?'

He almost snorted at the thought but was glad he didn't when the room remained quiet.

'I came by the other day just to check on your nephew and make sure he had everything he needed—and he told me he's a bit worried about you, Salvador.'

Salvador? The use of his first name transported him back to his childhood days, when he'd known he was in trouble if his mother used his full name on him. His eyes darted to Felix, who was suddenly very interested in seeing what pattern was printed on the back of the playing cards.

'I thought you were a bit distracted myself when I last saw you after transferring Henrique Orlay to a long-term care team.' The mention of the patient drove a sharp pain in between his ribs, and he hid a wince.

It happened a lot as he walked around the hospital, passing places he and Yara had spent time together or talking to people who had been on the case and hearing their admiration of her. Yara had been at this hospital for only two weeks but somehow the corridors were imbued with her memory, everything evoking a sense of familiarity and home in his chest—followed by mind-numbing pain that surpassed what he'd gone through the first time she left by several orders of magnitude.

Last time Salvador believed something significant in him had broken. Now he knew that it couldn't be repaired. He would be less than whole for ever, because that one piece of him belonged to her—no matter if they were together or not.

'I spoke to your colleagues as well, and they expressed similar observations ever since…' Chief Sakamoto didn't finish his sentence, instead looking at Felix, who finally stopped shuffling the cards around in his hands to face his uncle.

'Tio, you miss Yara, don't you?' Felix asked.

Salvador's mouth fell open—at the sheer bluntness of the boy and how much he had observed about him. Had he somehow picked up on the depth of his feelings for Yara? How was that even possible? Before his accident, they had never even met.

'I…don't see how that's at all relevant,' he replied, and didn't like the way his voice wavered—or how Felix and the Chief exchanged a knowing look. 'And I don't see how this is any of your concern. I've been doing my job, haven't I?'

'Martins, you've been as exemplary as ever—and yet your nephew wasn't the only one who noticed something off about you. It was questions from your colleagues that prompted me to seek out Felix. They said you were so heart-broken that I feared something awful had happened here.'

'Something awful *did* happen here.' The words flew out of his mouth, and rapid breaths expanded his chest as he probed for the deep and hidden place the words had come from. 'She's gone again.'

Chief Sakamoto exchanged another loaded look with Felix, a sensitivity beyond the boy's years shining in his eyes as he nodded, a voice-less message passing between them.

'Seems we just got to the bottom of this. Felix said it had most likely to do with Dr Silvia.'

Salvador turned his head towards his nephew, his mouth pressed into a thin line. 'How could you know about her?'

The boy hesitated, his hands scrunching up the blanket on his legs. 'I don't want to get into trouble...'

'You're already in trouble, no matter what you say. Might as well speak your mind, *filho*.'

Son. A word that had been dancing on the tip of his tongue for several months, waiting for the moment when it felt *right* to say. Because he might be Felix's uncle, a title he cherished more than anything, but in this moment their connection ran a lot deeper. Hell, he'd been so worried about Salvador that he'd got the Chief involved. If he was going to tell him something, it would be now.

'You were much more relaxed in the last two weeks, much...happier. I thought Tio always seemed a bit sad, maybe because of Dad or because you had to take me in. But then suddenly you were happy again...' A pink flush appeared on Felix's cheeks, something Salvador would normally have found adorable if he hadn't been so stunned by what his nephew had shared with him.

'I'm sorry, Felix. You had so much to deal with, and it sounds like I made my unhappiness part of your burden.'

Felix had put up with his unhappiness, seeing it as clear as day when he had thought he was hiding it so well. The small kernel of regret inside him exploded, uncoiling its roots and digging deep into his flesh.

He thought he needed to sacrifice everything to keep Felix safe, and by doing so he had put all his misery on those young shoulders. It dawned on him that he needed to live his own life and weave it through the threads of Felix's, rather than stop existing just so he could watch over his nephew.

'I don't know how to make it right, but I will try. Yara, though… I think I drove her away for good. By now, she's probably halfway across the world.' Salvador's chest tightened more, making each breath a hard-fought battle. He'd made a mistake, and he didn't know what to do.

The Chief cleared his throat, drawing Salvador's attention to him. 'Well… I did offer her the chance to stay here and run her own department.'

'You did what?' Salvador stared at Chief

Sakamoto with wide eyes, the implication of his words just sinking in.

'She hasn't accepted it, but she hasn't refused it either. I asked her two days ago if she had an answer, and she asked for more time to think. So…she hasn't said no.'

She hadn't declined the Chief's offer? His pulse took a tumble, and when it found its rhythm again it increased in speed so much that Salvador could hear the blood rushing through his ears. She hadn't said no. Yara would have said no if she was hell-bent on leaving. She didn't play hard to get—in fact, he had been the one causing the problems between them.

'You think she's still here?' Was it possible that he could fix his mistake—or at least try? Take the words back before it was too late?

'Go and find her. Felix isn't going to be discharged until you're back. I'll make sure of that,' Chief Sakamoto said with a congenial smile. 'And when you do find her, tell her that I need an answer.'

Salvador hesitated a moment, looking at his nephew, who encouraged him with a nod as well. He took another deep breath and left, fumbling for his keys in his pocket. If Yara was still in Brasília, there was only one place she'd feel safe enough to let her guard down.

The scent of chamomile drifted into the living room, and Yara scrunched up her nose at it. The last few days had been a blur of tears, sleep and chamomile tea that her sister forced into her hand at every opportunity—to the point where she didn't want to see a single cup of that stuff for several more months.

There was no doubt about the healing properties of the plant, but there wasn't a cure for what Yara was experiencing—complete and utter heartbreak, to the point where it was hard to breathe.

It had taken several nights of take-aways and soothing nature sounds to work through what had happened between her and Salvador, something that still left her raw on the inside. She had found the courage to tell him she loved him, and, though there had always been a part of her that knew he might not say it back, she was still crestfallen when her worst-case scenario became a reality right in front of her.

'He doesn't love me back...' Yara mumbled,

making her sister look up from her crocheted blanket.

'We've been over this before, but I'll say it again—you *must* know that's not true. I saw you at Flávia's engagement party. Everyone did. He was practically worshipping you.' They had this exact conversation several times a day whenever Yara fell deeper into the hole of her own misery.

It just didn't make sense. If he loved her, why was she here right now, hiding in her sister's guest room until she could think about the future again? Because without even planning, her perception of her life had changed, and she had created space for Salvador and whatever family they were going to become.

'My neighbours are already collecting money to get another permit for a party because they are certain you and Salvador are going to be next,' Bianca continued, and Yara snorted at that suggestion.

'I'm never getting married again. It hasn't ended well for me,' she grumbled.

'Don't you think that might be the problem and why Salvador ultimately said he couldn't be with you?'

'What? Because I don't want to marry him?' She glared at her sister, ignoring the indignant look on her face.

'No, that you say marriage didn't end well for you when that's not true. Marrying *Lawrence* didn't end well for you. It has nothing to do with marriage itself. But you cling to that thought and wield it like a shield around you. Maybe Salvador really wanted to be with you, but you were too worried about protecting yourself from the perceived threats of marriage.'

Yara recoiled at the intensity of her sister's words, her lips parting in an instant rebuttal that died in her before she could voice it. A sharp pinch in her chest stopped her from saying anything, and a cold sense of dread pooled at the bottom of her stomach. The truth of Bianca's words hit her like a wall of bricks, crashing down on her until they were too heavy for her to breathe.

'I…thought he loved me too. When our parents were so happy about my relationship, I thought I had everything I needed to move on—that we would learn to truly love each other with time.' She had carried those words inside her for so long, her shoulders sagged with relief as the weight lifted off. 'I turned my back on Salvador because I thought Mum and Dad knew best, that they would never push me in a direction that wasn't the right one for *me*.'

Bianca put her blanket aside and moved to the spot on the couch next to her, putting an arm around her shoulder. 'I'm sorry you suffered so much, but the only person telling you who you should be with now is you.'

'No wonder Salvador couldn't say it back. He's only ever known me as a person easy to influence. I've never shown him that I'm ready to do anything to make this happen—that I no longer run.' She looked at her sister with wide eyes as the realisation hit her. She had done exactly the same thing she'd done thirty years ago—she'd walked out on him without putting up a fight.

'What do you want to do?' Bianca asked.

'I can't just expect him to say it,' Yara said, shaking her head. 'I have to fight for it.'

A grin spread over her sister's face. 'That sounds a lot more like my big sister.'

Yara got up and looked around, her mind kicking into action mode the way it did when she was doing her initial diagnosis. 'I have to go to him.'

'Yes!' Bianca jumped up with her and walked into the kitchen before returning with her car keys, throwing them at her sister. 'Take my car. It's faster than waiting for a taxi.'

Yara gripped the keys, holding them to her heaving chest, and nodded at Bianca. She forced herself to take each step of the staircase with deliberation when everything inside her urged her to take them two at a time. Salvador was not going to go anywhere. He might even stick to his previous conviction, but she wouldn't let it stand without a fight. He was worth a thousand battles, if that was what it took to show her sincerity and love.

She flung the door open—and stood face to face with Salvador, his hand raised in an imminent knock.

His gaze bored into hers, an undeniable spark in his eyes that brought an unexpected weakness to her knees. 'What are you doing here?' she whispered.

'I was coming to see you.'

'Weird. I was doing the same thing.'

'That *is* weird.' Salvador chuckled, and the

sound vibrated through her, finding its way into her core and lighting a gentle fire there.

'Salvador, I—' She didn't get much further before he pulled her into his arms, crushing her against his chest in an embrace that conveyed everything words couldn't. He kissed the crown of her head, his hands clutching at her as if she was his lifeline, saving him from treacherous waves.

'Let me go first, because I need to say something I should have said ages ago. I love you, Yara. All of you, without compromise. I don't care about anything else but being with you.'

The words she'd been yearning to hear rang in her ears, threatening to rob her of any remaining composure. She tilted her head back and shuddered when he obliged her silent plea, brushing his lips over hers. Her knees turned to rubber under the kiss she'd been longing for since their conversation in the hospital.

The piece that went missing thirty years ago slotted back into place, a warm wholeness radiating through her entire body as she leaned against his chest. When he finally let go of her lips, she looked up at him and saw that same wholeness reflected at her.

'How is Felix?' she asked, and the smile on his lips further weakened her already unsteady legs.

'I love that you're asking about him first.' His hand came up to her face, brushing over her cheekbone. 'He's fine. Actually, he was the one who made me realise what a huge mistake I'd made.'

Yara remembered what Felix had said to her as well—that Salvador finally seemed happy again. 'What a smart boy you have.'

'Yeah, we do.' He paused, only a slight hesitation in his words, as if he was afraid what her reaction would be. 'I wasn't being considerate of your experience, thinking that we can only be a family in one specific way—when that couldn't be further from the truth.'

Yara shook her head. 'I shouldn't have left again. Not without putting up more of a fight. That's why I was rushing out of the house to come and talk to you. What happened to me with my marriage scared me so much, it blinded me to what else could be waiting out there.'

His arms tightened around her as she pressed her cheek against his chest. His lips moved over the crown of her head again, each spoken word becoming a gentle kiss. 'I don't need anything more from you than this right here, Yara. Everything else we can figure out.'

'Even if I don't want to get married?' She swallowed the lump in her throat.

'I don't care about any of that, *amor*. If we get married or not, if you want to keep travelling around the world—you and I are what matter here.'

'Salvador...' Her eyes burned with tears she blinked away. Here he was standing in front of her, telling her with a steadfast belief that they could be together no matter what—something she wished she had believed thirty years ago. She would not waste this second chance she'd received.

'I'm staying,' she said, and sensed the tremble in his body. 'Dr Sakamoto offered me my own department. He wants his hospital to become *the* diagnostic centre in Brazil.'

'I could never ask you to stay here if you don't...'

Yara shook her head, raising her face towards his once more. 'This is what I want. I want you and Felix together here in our home.'

CHAPTER THIRTEEN

'THIS IS ONLY a mild case of encephalitis. Who sent me this file? Neurology should be able to diagnose this by themselves.'

Yara looked up from her screen and saw Salvador standing in her doorway, arms crossed in front of his chest—an amused smile curling his lips. He smiled a lot more these days, something she had noticed ever since they'd moved in together to his house in Planaltina. After speaking to Felix about what had happened on the night he ended up in the hospital, as well as what was going on between Yara and Salvador, they decided a fresh start all round would be the best way forward.

Felix's new school was within walking distance from their house, and small enough so they knew everyone in his class.

Months had passed since then, with Yara working tirelessly to grow her diagnostic department to the size she needed to run it on a larger scale. Sometimes she missed her solo practice and her adventures travelling around the world—until she saw Salvador standing in front of her like that and everything faded into the background.

'I thought it made for an interesting scan for your trainees, so I sent it up. Excuse me for causing offence, Dr Lopes.' His tone didn't match his words, a playful lilt accompanying everything.

Yara got off her chair, looking at Salvador first, before her eyes drifted to the name on her door: *Dr Yara Lopes, Head of Diagnostics.*

Another step she had to thank him for. For the longest time she'd believed her married name to be intrinsically linked to her professional success, fearing that people would stop recognising her work or her abilities if she took that final step to absolve herself from her failed marriage.

'Is it already time?' she asked, buried so deeply in different cases that time had passed her by unnoticed.

'It's okay. I'm sure no one will notice if we are late to our own party,' he quipped, earning him a playful slap on the shoulder.

He caught her left hand, taking it in his own and looking at it with a reverence that caused a shiver to trickle through her body. Their eyes locked for a heartbeat, then he lowered his lips to her fingers and kissed the delicate white-gold ring on her ring finger.

'Let's go,' she said, wrapping her hand around his and pulling him out of her office.

As it turned out, her old neighbourhood had been right to collect money to pay for the next party permit—and that it was Yara and Salvador who would be celebrating.

'Did you hear anything from your mother?' he asked as they stepped out, and Yara shook her head.

'Yes, she'll be there. I hope once things quieten down we can have some time to talk things through,' Yara said, shrugging when Salvador's concerned gaze met hers.

'I'm fine, *amor*. Besides, Bianca will be there to help her understand.' She leaned in and whispered near his ear, her lips grazing over his skin as she spoke. 'You don't have anything to worry about. I have you, don't I?'

* * * * *

LET'S TALK
Romance

For exclusive extracts, competitions
and special offers, find us online:

f facebook.com/millsandboon

◉ @millsandboonuk

🐦 @millsandboon

Or get in touch on 0844 844 1351*

For all the latest titles coming soon,
visit millsandboon.co.uk/nextmonth